T5-DHH-948

LITTLE LIES

AUDREY JOHNSON

SCHOLASTIC INC.
New York Toronto London Auckland Sydney

Cover photograph by **Bernard Vidal**

ISBN 0-590-33492-1

12 11 10 9 8 7 6 5 4   9/8 0 1 2 3/9

Printed in the U.S.A.   01

LITTLE LIES

A Wildfire Book

WILDFIRE TITLES FROM SCHOLASTIC

Love Comes to Anne by Lucille S. Warner
I'm Christy by Maud Johnson
Beautiful Girl by Elisabeth Ogilvie
Superflirt by Helen Cavanagh
Dreams Can Come True by Jane Claypool Miner
I've Got a Crush on You by Carol Stanley
An April Love Story by Caroline B. Cooney
Dance with Me by Winifred Madison
Yours Truly, Love, Janie by Ann Reit
The Summer of the Sky-Blue Bikini by Jill Ross Klevin
The Best of Friends by Jill Ross Klevin
The Voices of Julie by Joan Oppenheimer
Second Best by Helen Cavanagh
A Place for Me by Helen Cavanagh
Sixteen Can Be Sweet by Maud Johnson
Take Care of My Girl by Carol Stanley
Lisa by Arlene Hale
Secret Love by Barbara Steiner
Nancy & Nick by Caroline B. Cooney
Wildfire Double Romance by Diane McClure Jones
Senior Class by Jane Claypool Miner
Cindy by Deborah Kent
Too Young to Know by Elisabeth Ogilvie
Junior Prom by Patricia Aks
Saturday Night Date by Maud Johnson
He Loves Me Not by Caroline Cooney
Good-bye, Pretty One by Lucille S. Warner
Just a Summer Girl by Helen Cavanagh
The Impossible Love by Arlene Hale
Sing About Us by Winifred Madison
The Searching Heart by Barbara Steiner
Write Every Day by Janet Quin-Harkin
Christy's Choice by Maud Johnson
The Wrong Boy by Carol Stanley
Make a Wish by Nancy Smiler Levinson
The Boy for Me by Jane Claypool Miner
Class Ring by Josephine Wunsch
Phone Calls by Ann Reit
Just You and Me by Ann Martin
Homecoming Queen by Winifred Madison
Holly in Love by Caroline B. Cooney
Spring Love by Jennifer Sarasin
No Boys? by McClure Jones
Blind Date by Priscilla Maynard
That Other Girl by Conrad Nowels
Little Lies by Audrey Johnson

CHAPTER ONE _____

The two little boys I was caring for this summer watched me build a sand castle on the beach. This was the third week of my summer vacation and I was enjoying myself. The beach was my world — the surf, the ocean breeze, and the sun pouring down like melted butter over the hot sand.

I dug deeper to reach the wet sand and scooped up handfuls to form a tower. Then I dug a trench around the castle. "This is a moat," I explained. "In olden days people built them around castles to keep their enemies out. You can get some water in your pail and fill the moat."

"How did people get into the castle?" asked four-year-old Scott. "Did they swim across?"

"No, they used a drawbridge they could raise or lower." I picked up a small piece of driftwood and laid it across the moat. "When the drawbridge was down, they could move their soldiers, horses, and supplies across it."

When Scott trotted off to get some water, I realized with a start that Robbie, who was almost two, was gone. The next thing I knew, a pair of muscular brown legs flashed past me and I saw a tall boy in white swim trunks scoop Robbie up where he was floundering in half a foot of water.

"Oh, no!" I cried. "Is he all right?"

"As good as new," the boy answered, carrying Robbie back and sitting him down beside me on the sand. Robbie was crying and I picked him up and held him on my lap, trying to reassure him.

I felt weak with relief. "He could have drowned! I only took my eyes off him for a minute!"

"You know how fast little kids can move. When they're this little you can't take anything for granted."

"Believe me, I know! This isn't the first time Robbie has given me a scare. Thank you for coming to the rescue. I'm Shannon McCabe."

"I'm Blake Harrison," he answered, sitting down on the sand beside me. "Are you here for the summer?"

I nodded, noting how good-looking he was. Dark brown hair framed a slim, tanned face and his dark eyes regarded me as if he liked what he saw.

"My brother and I have been biking around the country and we just arrived here yesterday. Do you come to the beach often?"

"Every day," I replied.

"That was a stupid question. You have a beautiful tan."

A nice line, I thought. He didn't waste any time. I could tell Blake wasn't just another biker riding around, looking for kicks. He had an air of confidence that comes from knowing who you are and where you're going.

"Where are you staying, Shannon?"

"With the Beaumonts." I hoped Blake would think I was a guest at this wealthy summer colony. I wanted to impress him, so I didn't tell I had been hired as a live-in baby-sitter for the summer. Even though Mrs. Beaumont referred to me as the "boys' companion," I was still the nursemaid, there so that she could play golf, entertain at the Yacht Club, or volunteer for local projects such as preserving historical landmarks — of which Cape Cod had plenty.

Blake stretched out on his back and regarded me thoughtfully. "Where are you from?"

"A little suburb you've never heard of."

"Try me."

I shook my head. I wouldn't mention my dreary little hometown. It had become practically a disaster area since its main industry — Harris Instruments — had merged with another company and moved out of town.

"Where do you go to school?" he asked.

I was pretty sure Blake was just passing through and I would never see him again after this afternoon. I might as well have

3

a little fun. "I go to Sunderlin's," I answered casually, mentioning an exclusive girls' school I had once read about in *The New York Times*. The public school I actually went to was operating on a strict budget and was eliminating the art and music departments next year. Even the sports program was threatened.

"I've heard of Sunderlin's," he answered.

"Are you in college?" I asked.

"I've been accepted at Boston University this fall. I'm majoring in journalism. I'm sure the field is overcrowded but I like a challenge. I'll just have to work harder."

"Have you done any writing?"

"The school paper, a couple stories in literary magazines, a sports column in a weekly newspaper."

"I'm impressed."

He laughed. "You shouldn't be. Have you picked your college?"

"I'm a senior. I've picked my college, but I don't know if they will pick me. I'd like to major in film at Hunter College in New York." I wasn't putting Blake on. I was interested in a career in photography and filming.

He raised up on an elbow. "Film? You mean motion pictures?"

"There are other aspects of filming — commercials, visual aids, documentaries, safety education films, government filming."

"Now it's my turn to be impressed. Most of the girls I know want to be models."

"Come on, Blake. That sounds pretty sexist. Not every girl wants to be a model."

"Well, maybe a few want to go into social work or politics." He grinned. "Do you think you could get me into the movies when you're successful? Maybe as a stand-in for Robert Redford?"

"You're making fun of me. I didn't laugh when you said you wanted to be a writer."

"I'm sorry, Shannon," he said, seriously. "I shouldn't have teased you. I like to kid around and sometimes I hurt people's feelings without meaning to."

"I take my photography very seriously."

"I will, too, from now on. Am I forgiven?"

"For the time being." I found Blake easy to talk to and we discussed music and tennis and our favorite authors.

Finally Blake said, "Did you know that Robbie is asleep? I'll spread out the beach towel for him." He shook the sand out of the towel and placed it on the sand. He lifted Robbie out of my arms and gently laid him down. Robbie lay with his little arms thrown back in complete abandon.

"That looks inviting. Do you mind if I stretch out, too? I'm beat. We didn't get in until after midnight last night," he said.

"Be our guest," I offered. "I'd take a nap, too, but I won't take my eyes off the boys. I've learned my lesson." Scott was playing in the wet sand by the water, digging holes with a stick, and watching the tide roll in and fill them.

5

Blake stretched out beside Robbie on the beach towel and closed his eyes. In a few minutes his deep, even breathing told me he was asleep.

I opened a new bottle of suntan lotion and applied it on my arms and legs. I would have liked to put some on Blake's back. His shoulders were as brown as leather and probably dry. I wondered what he would do if I rubbed some lotion on his back. I didn't know him well enough to try. I wished I had asked him where he was from and how long he was going to stay on the Cape.

I turned on my transistor radio and sat hugging my knees and watching the gulls ride the waves and then rise gently into the air. I thought about the circumstances that had brought me to Piedmont Point on Cape Cod. The affluence of this wealthy summer resort often overwhelmed me. For me, it was an entirely different world.

Last summer I had gone to a tennis camp in Connecticut and I had planned to go again this year. Then my dad lost his management job when Harris Instruments merged three months ago; and he was unsuccessful in his attempts to find another job in his line of work. His severance pay would soon be exhausted and sometimes our home seemed like an armed camp, with my parents arguing about money. Fear and worry made them lash out at each other.

Even before my father spoke to me one evening in May when we were setting out

marigold plants along the front of the house,
I had decided to get a job for the summer.
We took the garden tools back into the ga-
rage, and Dad rinsed his hands off with the
garden hose.

I knew there was something on his mind.
Finally, he cleared his throat. "Shannon, I
don't know how I can send you to tennis
camp and Ben to Scout camp this summer. I
just don't have the money."

"No sweat. I've decided to get a job." I put
the spade and the rake away.

"You had your heart set on going to camp
with your friends."

"It's all right. I'm not such a hot tennis
player. Do you think you could manage
Ben's camp fee? It's only half of what my
camp would have cost."

"I think we could, but that wouldn't be
fair to you." My father looked concerned.

"Ben's working hard toward his Eagle
Scout. Let's give him a break. He could fill
some of the requirements this summer at
camp." My fourteen-year-old brother's asth-
matic condition prevented him from par-
ticipating in vigorous sports, but he did have
his heart set on becoming an Eagle Scout.
"I've got a little money saved if he needs any
special gear."

I didn't want a halo. You did what you had
to do, and my brother had more need of
camp than I did. I looked around for a summer job. There were openings at the fast
food chains but I didn't want to spend the

summer bagging French fries and wiping off counter tops.

I found my job unexpectedly through Miss Linn, my guidance counselor at school, who knew Mrs. Beaumont from college and still corresponded with her. Mrs. Beaumont asked her if she could recommend a reliable high school girl who would live in and baby-sit at the family summer home on Cape Cod.

It wasn't a bad life. The pay equaled what I would have earned at a restaurant, and I had Thursdays and every other weekend off. Any evening when the Beaumonts were home and not entertaining was free. I had complete charge of the little boys. I bathed and fed them, made sure they took their naps, and supervised every moment of their waking hours.

In the spacious summer home I had my own bedroom — a bright, airy room that overlooked the ocean. On my days off, I took my camera and photographed the sand dunes, the fishing boats, and the stately houses with their widows' walks on the roof-tops, where the wives of whalers long ago watched for the return of their seafaring husbands. I took countless pictures of Robbie and Scott, who were perfect subjects.

And here I was now, sitting on the beach with one of the most interesting boys I had ever met. I wondered how long he was going to sleep. I wished he would wake up so we could talk some more.

In the distance I saw a lone jogger loping

along the beach. I would recognize Ryan Webster's tall, lanky form anywhere. Ryan was a townie, one of the local boys I had met who lived on the Cape the year round. We shared an interest in photography, but we were just friends.

I didn't want him to see me with Blake. He might mention my baby-sitting job. I bent my head as if I were looking for something in the sand, but I wasn't lucky. "Hi, Ryan!" Scott called. "Shannon's over here!"

The little boy came running over, kicking sand in Blake's face, and waking him up. "Ryan's coming!" he announced. Ryan was a favorite of Scott's. They played Frisbee together.

Blake sat up, brushing the sand off his face. "What's going on?"

Ryan surveyed us. "Well, as usual, Blake, I see you've zeroed in on the best-looking girl on the beach."

Blake drawled, "Why, it's my old friend, Bones. Tell me, man, are you still playing tin soldier?" Last summer Ryan had had a job at the historical fort in the area. A well-known tourist trap, it hired high school and college students to dress up as British and American soldiers and stage mock Revolutionary War battles for the benefit of the tourists.

Apprehension grabbed at me. Blake and Ryan knew each other! Did that mean Blake was a resident of the summer colony?

"No," Ryan replied. "I'm playing boat captain this year."

9

"For that ramshackle tour boat enterprise of your uncle's?"

"That's the one." Ryan was playing it cool.

"Someday that tour boat is going to spring a leak and sink. Have you added life preservers yet?" Blake grinned.

I found my voice. "How do you two know each other?"

"I've been beating on him ever since he was ten years old," Ryan replied.

"Not last year. You couldn't catch me. Remember?"

Ryan was smiling. "I hope you notice I'm in training this year. I run five miles every day."

They were both laughing, and Ryan turned to me. "It's not as bad as you think, Shannon. The summer jocks would be disappointed if we didn't pick fights. It's part of our summer recreation."

Blake looked at his watch. "I hate to break up this intellectual discussion but I promised my brother I'd go sailing with him. We haven't had the boat out all summer." He turned to me. "Are you going to be on the beach tomorrow, Shannon?"

I was in luck. Tomorrow was my day off. "I'll be here."

"I'll see you then." He paused. "Shannon, leave the kids at home. Okay?"

I should have told him right then and there I was employed by the Beaumonts and not their house guest, but I was so pleased a boy like Blake was interested in me and

10

wanted to see me again. It might end in disaster but I could continue my hoax, at least for tomorrow.

I watched him leave. "Does Blake live around here?"

"Sure, that's Blake Harrison. See that big house down on the point?" Ryan answered.

Harrison. I should have recognized the name. The house was a showplace and even Mrs. Beaumont had pointed it out to me. The lawn looked like a green velvet sea surrounding a great white house. In this land of sand, I wondered how the gardeners maintained that green, green lawn.

Blake was going to find me out. It was just a matter of time, but, please, let me have tomorrow with him, I thought. Then I'll tell him.

It was time to gather up the boys and head for home. Mrs. Beaumont liked us home by four o'clock so the boys could have their baths and an early supper. Robbie was still groggy when we woke him and Ryan offered to carry him home. I gathered up the beach paraphernalia and called Scott, who was on his stomach examining a strange-looking bug he wanted to take home.

"I should have brought the stroller but Robbie refuses to ride in it anymore. He also refuses to walk when he is tired."

"I was going to ask you to ride on the tour boat with me tomorrow. You could have sat up front and kept me company."

"I'm sorry, Ryan. Try me another time."

"You think Blake's a pretty nice guy, don't you?"

"He seems nice," I admitted.

"What does he have that I don't have — besides being handsome, rich, and Mr. Personality personified?" Ryan joked. But I knew he was challenging me.

"Come on, Ryan. You have a lot going for you," I protested.

"Like what? I'm interested."

"Are you fishing for compliments? Let me see ..." I paused.

"See! You can't think of a single thing!"

"Sure I can. I just need time to think. You're nice to old ladies. I've seen you help the senior citizens on the tour boat. You're good with little kids. Robbie and Scottie adore you."

"Don't put me on. None of that counts with girls," he said gloomily.

"You're important to me. You're the first friend I made on the Cape this summer, Ryan. I mean that."

"Just once I wish you would look at me the way you looked at Blake when he asked you if you were going to be on the beach tomorrow."

"Did you really fight him every summer?" I asked.

"We townies outnumbered the summer kids, but sometimes we let them play. After all, they owned the motorbikes and the new basketballs. Blake's not a bad guy but he drives as if he's competing in the Grand Prix. Do you have your driver's license?"

12

"I passed driver's ed. this spring — but don't expect me to race Blake."

Ryan carried Robbie up the porch steps and placed him on a yellow-and-green lounge chair. Robbie immediately set up a howl. With his blond curls he usually looked like a Christmas tree cherub but when he was tired, not even Santa Claus could make him smile.

"By the way, Shannon, I'm going to ask my science teacher, Mr. Manning, if we can use his darkroom to develop our film. All we would have to buy are the supplies."

"That's great! We could save tons of money," I answered happily.

"Are you sure you'll know how to develop if we invest money for supplies?"

"Is the Pope Catholic?" I asked.

He smiled. "All right, Shannon. I'll see you around."

CHAPTER TWO _____

It took me a long time to fall asleep that night. All I could think about was Blake. I planned how I would tell him the truth tomorrow. At just the right moment I would say, "I was just joking yesterday. I'm really the Beaumonts' baby-sitter and Sunderlin's School for Girls is just a place I read about."

I was sure Blake would understand. He'd take my hand and say, "Shannon, do you really think that matters? It's you I'm attracted to — not your family or a prestigious school." It sounded great in the darkness of my bedroom, and I felt more at ease.

Ryan, on the other hand, was just a good friend. I'd met him one afternoon while I was out near the salt marshes photographing an old wooden bridge. He came jogging along but stopped when he realized he was coming into my camera's line of vision. I motioned for him to go on, that I was through, but instead he came over.

He was easily over six feet tall, his blue eyes were direct, and his hair a sunstreaked blond thatch. "What kind of a camera are you using?" he asked.

"A single lens reflex."

He noticed the make of the camera. "You didn't get this by collecting cereal tops. How long have you been interested in photography?"

"Ever since I knew how to press a button," I said. "Two years ago my grandparents wanted to give me a ten-speed bike for my birthday, but I persuaded them to get me a good camera."

"I've done some photography. Mostly action shots of sports events. Photographing wildlife interests me, too." He paused. "You're one of the summer people, aren't you?"

"How can you tell?"

"I can tell," he answered seriously.

I studied him. "I'll bet you're a basketball player."

"It's not an all-consuming interest with me. My coach thinks I'll get an athletic scholarship for college, but what I'm really interested in is oceanography."

"Right on target," I answered. "That's a great field."

"I think so, too," Ryan said. "I'm piloting a tour boat for my uncle this summer. It's the Red Star line and we're docked down

15

at the pier. If you'd like a free ride sometime, stop by. We make two trips daily
around the bay and we also charter tours
for special trips."

"I may take you up on that."

"Bring your camera. Our regular tours
cover most of the high spots."

"I'd rather find my subjects off the beaten
path," I said.

"I understand. Anyone can take pictures
of the Kennedy compound at Hyannisport."

Ryan and I became good friends, and on
my days off we roamed about, visiting the
Audubon Wildlife Sanctuary where he took
dozens of pictures. I liked the lonely beaches
where I found old wrecks abandoned high
and dry. I photographed them, experiment-
ing with aperture and filters for the best possible effects.

Ryan was comfortable to be with; not exciting or challenging like Blake, but with
Ryan I could just be myself. I didn't worry
about whether my eye makeup was running
or if my face was breaking out.

After meeting Blake on the beach that
day, I was so hyper I thought I would never
fall asleep. When I finally did, I dreamed of
Blake and Ryan, dressed in suits of armor,
storming a castle to gain my love. But someone raised the drawbridge and they both fell
into the water.

The next morning I awoke with the glori-
ous feeling I had the whole day to myself.
No rinsing out sandy swimming trunks, re-

trieving Scottie's stuffed animal — Poo Dog — from the surf, or wiping up spilled milk and cookie crumbs. I wondered if Blake had any special plans for the day.

Mrs. Beaumont called me from her room as I was going downstairs. She was petite, dark-haired, very competent, very self-assured. Some clothing was laid out on her bed. "You must wear about a size ten, Shannon," she said.

"Yes." Was she checking me out before she sent a bundle to the Salvation Army?

"If you won't feel offended, I have a few things I can't squeeze into this summer. I must have put on a few pounds."

She had to be kidding me. She was as slim as a reed and she watched her diet like an eagle scouting for prey.

She held up two pairs of beautifully tailored designer jeans and some great-looking tops. "Take these shorts, too. It just breaks my heart I can't get into them."

I thanked her, happy as a clam with my new clothes. None of them looked as if they had been worn. My own summer wardrobe was pretty slim, and I hadn't had money to spend on clothes after I'd bought the camping gear for Ben.

"When I was hired, I thought you might want me to wear a uniform. You know, the kind with an apron and a ruffled cap like nannies wear in English movies."

"My dear, I wouldn't do that to a sixteen-year-old girl. All I ask is that you be neat and conduct yourself in a proper manner."

17

The new clothes didn't fool me. With my old clothes I wasn't portraying the right image for the family at Piedmont Point, and it was her way of helping me fit in.

Back in my room I found Mrs. Beaumont had guessed my size when I tried on the clothes. I'd have to shorten the jeans but otherwise they fit perfectly. If Blake ever asked me out I'd have something nice to wear.

I decided to wear a pair of the new shorts and a halter top and I'd hit the beach early in case Blake came looking for me.

I gathered up my beach bag and my radio and went downstairs, hoping to avoid Rose Marie, the buxom, gray-haired widow who presided over the kitchen.

I didn't escape her eagle eye. "All right, Shannon McCabe. You're not starting the day without breakfast."

"You know I'm not a breakfast person."

"I've read about you teenaged girls starving yourselves because you are afraid of getting fat. Anorexia nervosa, they call it."

"Come on, Rose Marie. I always eat a big dinner at night. All I ever want for breakfast is an English muffin and orange juice."

She sighed. "No one wants to eat a substantial breakfast anymore. They're all afraid of cholesterol, salt, white bread, sugar, and I don't know what else. I used to cook for families who wanted ham and eggs, home fries, pancakes, and sausage."

"I'm practically a vegetarian myself," I said. "Almost, not quite. I still eat fish and

18

chicken occasionally." I sat down at the kitchen table.

She took the orange juice out of the refrigerator and popped a muffin into the toaster-oven. "I don't know what happened to roast beef and rich gravy and lemon meringue pie. It's just no fun cooking anymore."

I sipped my orange juice as she buttered the muffin. "On my way to the farm market yesterday afternoon, I saw you on the beach with the Harrison boy."

"Blake seems nice. I'm meeting him today."

"He drives a car like he's mad at the whole world, but I've never heard of him getting into real trouble. At one time, the Harrisons owned all of Piedmont Point. Of course, that was generations ago. It's old money, going all the way back to whaling days."

"Old money, new money. It's not important. I just know Blake is fun to be with." I rose to leave. "Thanks for the breakfast."

I was just leaving the porch when Mrs. Beaumont called to me. "Shannon, if you are just going to the beach, would you mind looking after the boys for a while? Their grandparents are on their way over to take them for the day."

What could I say? Scott and Robbie came out of the house, and I shepherded them across the road and over to the beach. I wasn't sure what I would tell Blake if he came along.

The beach was nearly deserted this early in the day, and I spread my beach towel on the sand and sat down. I took a paperback

19

novel out of my bag and tried to read. The words didn't mean a thing. I kept glancing up, watching for Blake.

The beach was wide and curving and the sun a molten red, forecasting a day of smothering heat. On the horizon a few points of white marked an occasional sailboat out for an early morning run.

A deeply tanned girl in a blue bathing suit, carrying a polka-dotted beach bag, came walking over the sand with two red-haired little girls. She smiled at us and spread a blanket on the beach a few yards away. The children kicked off their beach clogs and raced toward the water.

The girl sat down with her back toward us and I couldn't help noticing that she had a small butterfly tattooed on her shoulder blade.

To my embarrassment Robbie trotted over and stared at the tattoo. "Robbie," I called softly. "Come back here."

He pointed to the tattoo. "Sha-na-na! Bug! Bug!"

"Robbie!" I called sharply.

The girl was laughing as she turned around. She had an open, friendly face.

"I'm sorry," I apologized.

"It's a great conversation piece," she admitted.

"I'm sure it is."

"You'd be surprised how many fascinating boys I've met because of it. They all ask me why I had it done."

"I was trying to get up the nerve to ask you myself," I smiled.

"I wanted to be different. All my friends were getting their ears pierced."

She might be a little weird but I liked her. "Do you think you'll ever be sorry you had it done?"

"I haven't been sorry yet. Maybe when I'm seventy, people will do a double take when they see a butterfly on my wrinkled shoulder."

We were both laughing. I introduced myself. "I'm Shannon McCabe."

"I like Sha-na-na better. I'm Jamie Campbell."

"Are you baby-sitting for the girls?"

"I baby-sit occasionally for Mrs. Kingsley. This is the day she volunteers at the day care center. Weekends I'm a lifeguard at the YWCA pool."

"Where are you from?" I asked.

"I live here the year round. My grandfather calls us townies the Keepers of the Cape. How do you like working for the Beaumonts?"

"No complaints. Do you know Blake Harrison?"

"Ahah! You've met our tawny golden boy and you're impressed!" she exclaimed.

"Then you do know him?"

"All my life . . . that is, every summer of my life. I taught Blake to dig for clams."

Then I saw him coming along the beach, bronzed and muscular, as if he had just stepped out of a travel poster from some exotic vacation spot like Crete or Rhodes.

"Hi, Shannon. Hi, Jamie. What's Mac doing this summer?" he asked.

"He's painting houses. I think he's scheduled to paint yours in August." Jamie turned to me. "Mac is my boyfriend."

Blake flopped down on the sand beside me and raised himself on one elbow, "You're even more beautiful in the morning, Shannon. How many women can say that?"

"Most women under twenty," I said glibly.

Jamie snickered. Blake ignored her. "I like long hair. Don't ever cut yours."

"I'm always threatening to cut it in the summer," I admitted.

"What would you like to do today? Go sailing?"

"Sailing sounds like fun." I had never sailed before but I wouldn't admit it.

"Right on! Are you a good sailor?"

"I don't know how much help I'll be." How true!

Robbie came running up to Blake. "Frisbee! Frisbee!"

Blake reached over and tousled Robbie's blond hair. "Maybe tomorrow, sport." He was frowning as he turned back to me. "Don't tell me you're watching the kids again today? We can't take them out in the sailboat!"

"Don't get excited. The boys' grandparents are picking them up for the day."

"That's better. I know you must like little kids, but big boys are more fun."

I smiled. "I'm sure they are."

"You might want to stop home and get some warm clothing. The weather's pretty unpredictable and it could be chilly out on the water."

"I have a sweat shirt in my bag. I usually carry one because it gets cold, even on the beach."

"You'll need sneakers, too. We may have an extra pair in the boathouse." He looked toward the road. "Are those people trying to get your attention? They keep waving."

Robbie and Scott spotted their grandparents at the same time, and, shrieking with delight, they ran toward them. Mrs. Beaumont said the grandparents spoiled them outrageously.

We said good-bye to Jamie and walked along the road toward the big white house on the point. The house looked like a ship riding on the green sea of grass. As we drew nearer I could see the carefully attended flower gardens, and surrounded by manicured shrubbery was a statue of Diana, the goddess of hunting. I wondered if Blake would take me inside to introduce me to his parents but he didn't. Instead we crossed the lawn and went down several flights of steps to the dock where a sailboat was moored next to a large cabin cruiser. Several smaller boats bobbed gently alongside.

Blake went into the boathouse and came out with a pair of men's sneakers, which were way too big, and we laughed as I clomped about in them.

I climbed in the boat and sat down where Blake told me to sit. "Don't be concerned with trying to make yourself useful if you don't know what you're doing. You might just get in the way."

As Blake prepared to cast off, the wind blew through the flapping sails with a two-toned sound like a chord on an electric guitar. Then we left the dock and my first reaction was one of unsteadiness as the boat tipped on its side. I felt an urge to move to a safer spot.

"Stay there!" Blake ordered. "And keep your eye on the boom!" The boom was a horizontal bar almost as long as the boat. "Duck when I yell, 'Ready about, hard alee.' The boom could knock you right out of the boat."

We moved out into the open water and I relaxed a little. The water sparkled around us, and I noticed how quietly the sails performed now that we were moving. We passed other sailboats, weaving in and around them in a symphony of motion. The air was cool and I dug my sweat shirt out of my beach bag and put it on.

Blake at the helm didn't pay much attention to me except to shout orders. He nearly threw a fit when I rested my feet on a coil of rope. "If the rope runs out in a hurry it could wrap around your ankles and take the skin off!" Just as suddenly he would yell, "Weather side!" which ordered me to the opposite side of the boat.

We moved up the coast, past little towns and a lighthouse built of stone, past the oyster harbors and an occasional windmill. After several hours of sailing, we entered a quiet little bay. "We're going to make a mooring here," he called back.

He dropped the jib sail and we headed for the dock. Attaching the mooring line, he secured the boat and offered me a hand. "You've never sailed before, have you?"

"No," I admitted.

"Before the summer is over I'll have you handling the boat alone."

"Sure you will," I replied skeptically.

"This is one of my favorite coves. I'll show you where my brother and I used to camp with my cousins when we were kids. You'd better put your sandals back on."

I took off the wet sneakers and slipped into my sandals. Holding hands, we walked along the pier and across the sand. We crossed a footbridge, a rustic combination of planks and log railings, and walked Indian file up a path that rose steadily through a stand of pine trees. The sun made moving patterns on the ground; the fragrance of the pines filled the air. It reminded me of a pillow my grandmother had that was filled with pine needles — a souvenir from a state park.

Then the path widened and we walked together, Blake's arm around me. A meadow opened beyond the trees, and he pointed to a grassy plateau presided over by a lone oak tree. "There's our camping ground. Old-timers say it's one of the highest points on the Cape."

When we reached the top, I paused to look

around. The view was breathtaking. The towns with their white church steeples looked like toy villages from a model railroad, and a wealth of scenery was spread out before us — awesome stretches of dunes, the magnificent white, sandy beaches. We sat down and rested awhile.

"I've never brought a girl here before, Shannon. That's how special I think you are."

Tell him now, my conscience urged me. You're not special. You're just a fake. But I kept silent.

"We had a pact, the four cousins, that this was off limits to girls." He smiled. "But that was long ago."

"You hauled your camping gear all the way up here?"

"It was worth it. And it was the nearest thing to complete freedom I've ever experienced. We set up camp under that tree and we swam and fished in the cove. We lived on fish and Twinkies and Kool-Aid and we never changed our clothes once."

I laughed. "My brother Ben is at Scout camp and he probably won't change his clothes, either."

"How long are you staying with the Beaumonts, Shannon?"

"For the rest of the summer."

"There's no one your age in the family. Are you a relative?"

"Sort of . . ." I murmured. I was getting to be an accomplished liar.

"What do you mean . . . sort of? You're

26

either a relative or you're not. Do you mean by marriage?"

"I guess you would call it that." This was terrible. I was getting in deeper and deeper, and the longer I waited the harder it was going to be to tell him. If I told him now we might quarrel, and it would end this day that was starting out so wonderfully.

"My parents play golf with the Beaumonts and they entertain back and forth several times during the summer."

My heart sank down to my knees and stayed there. Suppose Blake and his parents arrived for a dinner party and Blake asked where I was? Mrs. Beaumont would tell him I didn't dine with the family but ate with the boys at five o'clock. She might even tell him what a jewel I was as a mother's helper and they were so glad they'd found me.

Blake looked around. "I wonder if there are still blackberries growing along the woods. They should be ripe now. Come on, let's have a look."

He pulled me to my feet and we walked over to the edge of the woods. We found the bushes in the underbrush, heavy with berries. "My grandmother said berries have a habit of growing in the wildest, most abandoned places," I offered.

"Do you get poison ivy?"

"At least once a year," I admitted. "Unfortunately."

"You stay here. I'll pick the berries," he said.

"I wish we had something to put them in."

"We'll have to eat them," Blake answered.

"You'll get scratched up," I warned.

"That's half the price." Blake waded through the underbrush and came out with two handfuls of the shiny blackberries. I popped one in my mouth and the tangy sweetness was delicious. We ate all the berries and Blake went back for more.

We walked back and sat on the hillside to eat them. When we were finished our hands were stained and I took some Wash'n'Dries out of my bag and tried to scrub Blake's hands clean. The stain wouldn't come off. His arms and legs were scratched from the berry bushes, and I gently wiped the scratches.

I looked at my purple hands and was aware of how messy I must look.

"I'll bet my mouth is stained, too," I said, half to myself.

"It looks perfect," he replied. Then he reached over and kissed me. His lips were smooth and soft, just as I knew they would be, and I realized I had been waiting all day for him to kiss me. He drew me close, smoothing back my hair, then traced my lips with his finger. The sun winked off the gold beveling of his watch.

"Your lips are stained, too," I said softly. He didn't answer but kissed me again, this time a lasting kiss that made my breath come faster. I felt a rush of tenderness toward him, and I didn't want him to stop kissing me.

It was like a dream come true, being here

alone with a boy like Blake, almost a college man. It was easy to believe I was all the things I pretended to be — self-assured and poised from my exclusive schooling and wealthy family background.

He was holding me so close I could feel the pounding of his heart. A wave of feeling swept over me and I felt lost in space — like a carnival balloon floating in the sky.

Blake's kisses made me aware I had never really been kissed before. All those other kisses at school parties had been merely dress rehearsals.

Later we went swimming down at the cove, and I had to wear my shorts and halter top in the water because I didn't have my bathing suit along. We swam and clowned in the water and I watched Blake swim with strong, even strokes, his dark hair matted with water drops. He would swim underwater and come up under me unexpectedly. Of course, I knew it was Blake but I kept thinking of *Jaws* and it was unnerving. Finally, I escaped to the beach and watched the seagulls strutting along the wet sand, looking for clams as the tide went out.

The trip back home was uneventful and I could even help Blake a little when he shouted orders at me. "Will I see you tomorrow?" he asked as he moored the boat.

I had to work tomorrow. The noose was tightening around my neck. "Mrs. Beaumont is playing golf tomorrow — I said I'd watch the children for her."

"That won't take all day, will it?"

"Well, you know how it is. Lunch at the country club. Cocktails in the afternoon. She could make a day of it."

"For Pete's sake," he exploded. "Doesn't she ever take care of her own kids?"

"I don't mind."

"I think she's taking advantage of you. After all, you're a guest and she should be entertaining you, not exploiting you. We'll make a date for the weekend, then. Maybe a drive up to Provincetown?"

Everything was going wrong! This was my weekend off and my mother expected me home. I even had my bus ticket. I turned my head away. "I'd love to go to Provincetown. I've never been there! But, I'm going home this weekend."

He looked alarmed. "You're coming back?"

"Of course."

"I'll drive you home," he offered.

"I've already made arrangements." I was uneasy.

"Change them," he demanded.

"I don't want to."

He studied me and I grew uncomfortable under his direct gaze. "I don't understand you, Shannon. You came on strong for me this afternoon and now you act as if I have infectious hepatitis."

"You know that's not true." I reached up and kissed him. Then I ran for home.

CHAPTER THREE _____

I had really boxed myself in. I was falling into a trap that I had set myself. If I had leveled with Blake from the beginning, we would be building a beautiful relationship that wasn't based on deceit. Or would we?

Was Blake attracted to me because he thought I was on the same social level as he? Or wouldn't that have made any difference? One thing I was sure of: I had never felt this way about a boy before. Just thinking about him make a wonderful feeling steal over me. He had everything I wanted in a boy and so much more than that. He made all the other boys I knew seem immature.

The next morning as I prepared to go to the beach with the boys, Mrs. Beaumont said, "Don't forget the story hour at the library, Shannon."

Silently I groaned. I knew that Mrs. Mangus, the librarian, hated to see us come in.

Scott sat quietly through stories that had a lot of action or made him laugh, but about two minutes into a story, Robbie would start drumming his heels on the floor or turn around and make faces at the children behind him. Nothing on earth would make him stop, and Mrs. Mangus would glare at me until I left the room with him.

Today was no exception. We filed into the reading room, a small room off the main library, where about twenty children were waiting. I sat down on one of the kindergarten chairs and wondered what to do about my legs. Mrs. Mangus had visited Arizona once and bought a lot of Indian jewelry. She was wearing all of it today.

"Christmas!" Robbie said in a loud voice, pointing at her. Mrs. Mangus scowled.

Then she cleared her throat. "Children, I am going to read from an old favorite today — *Alice in Wonderland*." Someone groaned.

By the time Alice had met the rabbit, Robbie was humming in a loud voice. Mrs. Mangus stopped and stared hard at him. Then she stared hard at me. I took Robbie by the hand and we left the room. We walked down the corridors where he played with the drinking fountains, holding his hand over the stream of water until it splashed on the walls and floor.

The janitor was watching us, so I beat a hasty retreat with Robbie. Outside, the sun had burned away the morning haze, and the air was hot and humid. The dock was only a block away, and I wondered if Ryan was working. It might be cooler by the water.

Ryan was aboard his uncle's boat, the *Treasure Island*, polishing the brass railing. He wore cut-off jeans and was bare to the waist. He was so tanned I looked pale by comparison. "Hi," he called. "What's the occasion?"

"We were practically thrown out of the library and we have some time to kill."

"I need a break. Come on, I'll treat you and Robbie to Cokes. You have time, don't you?"

I glanced at my watch. "The story hour lasts about forty-five minutes."

We ordered Cokes at an outside table of a little restaurant. "How was your day with your preppy boyfriend?" Ryan asked.

"You mean Blake?" I played dumb.

"Who else?" He scowled.

"Just super."

"You look starry-eyed just mentioning his name."

I twirled the straw in my glass. "I did a really dumb thing and I don't know how to make it right."

"How come?"

"I gave Blake the impression I'm a guest at the Beaumonts'. He has no idea I'm the baby-sitter," I confessed.

"What's wrong? Are you ashamed of working?"

"Of course not. I was just playing around, and he believed me. He also thinks I go to an exclusive girls' school."

"You have a lot going for you, Shannon. You don't have to pretend you're someone else."

"Back home I knew who I was. I didn't have everything I wanted but neither did my friends. Here at Piedmont Point with the big homes and servants and kids my age with expensive sport cars and talking about trips to Europe, I feel out of step . . . sort of second-class."

"Hey, you're all wrong! Having money doesn't make a person any better."

"I know that. I just wanted to pretend for a little while, but now I'm in so deep I don't know how to get out," I said, feeling ashamed.

"You have to tell Blake. If he really cares for you it won't make any difference. If it does make a difference, he's not worth having for a friend."

"You've known him for a long time, Ryan. How do you think he'll take it?"

"I knew him as a kid. The last few summers I've been working and I haven't seen much of him. People change in their teens. You're not the same person you were when you were twelve."

I smiled ruefully. "No, I'm not."

He took my hand in his tanned one. "I wish I had known you when you were twelve, thirteen, fourteen." There was a gentleness in Ryan that touched me. I knew he cared for me and wanted to be more than a friend. I felt a little sad about it because no other boy could compare to Blake.

"My mother was always telling people I was the homeliest baby she had ever seen and she was embarrassed to show me. I made up my mind I was ugly and to compensate for it I tried to please. I wanted to be the brightest, the most athletic, the most talented girl in my class. I was an insufferable little eager beaver."

Ryan smiled. "Then, when you were older, you discovered that boys didn't think you were homely."

"Right — I would say about the time I reached junior high. I should have stopped knocking myself out, but I was already programed to try and be accepted by everyone. I still have times I'm unsure of myself and maybe that's why I wanted to impress Blake."

Ryan sat in silence, and for a long moment I didn't know if he was going to speak. Then he said, "I was five foot eleven in the seventh grade and people expected me to act as if I were eighteen. I felt out of step, too. Like a freak. Mentally and emotionally I was only a twelve-year-old kid. They called me Bones and made fun of me, so I withdrew." He sighed. "But sports helped. When my co-ordination caught up with my size, they found I wasn't a bad person to have on their team. But I've had my low points, too."

"I wish I could watch you play basketball sometime, Ryan."

He looked pleased. "Do you mean that? I could drive down and get you some Friday when we have a weekend game."

"It's ninety miles!" I cautioned.

"I wouldn't mind."

"I can just see my mother giving her permission!"

"You can stay at our house. My mother would be glad to call your mother to invite you," Ryan replied.

"I would probably have to bring my brother Ben along as chaperone."

Robbie had finished his Coke and was making slurping noises with his straw. "I've got to run, Ryan. The story hour will be letting out. Thanks for the Coke."

"We've never really talked before, Shannon."

"I know." Our eyes met with a warm understanding. If it weren't for Blake . . .

When I reached the library the story-hour room was deserted. The chairs were back in place and the books piled neatly on the table. I hurried over to the desk. "Where are the children?" I asked the library aide.

"They left about ten minutes ago," the girl answered. "Mrs. Mangus shortened the story hour because of the heat."

I felt a stab of apprehension. "Did you see a little blond boy leave the building?"

"I'm sorry, I didn't. I was busy checking out the children's books."

I ran outside and looked up and down the street but no children were in sight. I circled the building, thinking Scott might be waiting in the shade of the trees in the rear of the library. I was numb with panic. Had he wandered away, perhaps gone home with another child? Was he lost and confused, trying to find me?

I would need Ryan to help me search for him. I hurried down to the dock, carrying Robbie. "Ryan, I can't find Scott! The children have all left the building!"

He looked concerned. "Stay here with Robbie and I'll look in the school play yard."

Long moments passed as I waited nervously. He came back. "No, he isn't there. Do you suppose he went home?"

I was frantic. "It's three blocks," I almost shouted. "I don't know if he could find his way."

"He's a smart kid. That's probably just what he did when he couldn't find you. Come on. Let's check home before we look any farther. I'll carry Robbie."

Worry kept me silent as we hurried along the sidewalk. I should never have left Scott alone at the library. What would I tell Mrs. Beaumont?

As we neared the Beaumont residence, I saw her out on the veranda, looking up and down the street. Scott was at her side. I ran and hugged him, almost overcome with relief.

Mrs. Beaumont's face was etched in severity. "What is this all about? Scott came home alone. He said he couldn't find you."

"I'm sorry, Mrs. Beaumont. Robbie was disrupting the story hour and I left with him. When we came back, the children had been excused and I couldn't find Scott."

"Who is this young man?" She pointed to Ryan.

"Ryan Webster. He helped me search for Scott."

Ryan spoke up. "It's partly my fault, Mrs. Beaumont. I asked Shannon and Robbie to have a Coke with me."

The edges of her voice curled with disapproval. "Shannon wasn't hired to meet boys, young man. We pay her well to care for our children. When she is working we expect her to devote all her attention to them."

Ryan looked crestfallen and I felt mortified, both for myself and for him. Maybe I deserved a scolding, but couldn't she have done it in private without dragging Ryan into it?

"I'm sorry," he said. He excused himself and left.

I should have taken the job at Burger King, I said to myself. First had come the incident of Robbie floundering in the water on the beach. Now I had used poor judgment and Scott had had to find his way home alone. If anything had happened to the children, I would never have forgiven myself. Baby-sitting carried a lot of responsibility. Taking orders for hamburgers and chocolate milkshakes didn't risk other peoples' lives.

Mrs. Beaumont wasn't through with me. "I find this irresponsible and I intend to take it up with my husband this evening."

Maybe I would be fired.

"Another thing, Shannon. A young man called and left a message with Rose Marie this morning. I must ask you not to have your friends call you when you are working. Rose Marie is too busy to be your answering service."

CHAPTER FOUR _____

Still smarting from Mrs. Beaumont's scolding, I washed Robbie and supervised Scott's washing of his hands and face. "Mom was mad at you," Scott offered, wiping his hands and leaving most of the dirt on the towel. "She said I could have been kidnapped."

"Please, Scott, don't make me feel worse than I do."

"I found my way home all by myself. Robbie would have gotten lost."

I gave him a hug. "It won't happen again while I'm taking care of you. You know I wouldn't let anything happen to you."

I took the children downstairs for their lunch. Rose Marie had lunch set up on the white, iron-scrolled table in the screened-in porch off the dining room. Rose Marie looked at me with disapproval. "I heard Mrs. Beaumont hollering at you all the way back here. It's not like you to leave the boys alone."

"I tried to explain how it happened but I can't blame her for being angry. I just miscalculated the time."

"Well, luckily it turned out all right and no harm was done. Sit down and eat your sandwich and I'll make you some iced tea."

She busied herself with the ice cube tray. "You got a call while you were gone. Some boy who gave his name as Blake. Would that be Blake Harrison?"

"I don't know anyone else named Blake," I answered. "What did you tell him?"

"That you were at the library with the children."

"Did he leave a message?"

Rose Marie poured glasses of iced tea for both of us and sat down at the table. "No, he just thanked me and hung up. This is your weekend to go home, isn't it?"

"Yes. Maybe Mr. Beaumont will tell me not to come back. He's going to speak to me about what happened this morning."

"He's a pussycat. Don't worry about him. If anyone fires you, it will be Mrs. Beaumont. She wears the pants in the family, as my grandmother used to say. But I don't think they'll fire you. Good help is hard to find. Besides, Wednesday is the big party when they pay back all their social obligations and she won't want to break in a new baby-sitter."

"The party will make a lot of extra work for you, won't it?" I cut my sandwich in quarters and helped myself to some potato chips.

41

Rose Marie sniffed. "The food and service will be catered. Apparently, my cooking isn't good enough for the likes of the Harrisons, the Van Nesses, and the Forsyths."

My voice was a fearful whisper. "The Harrisons! They're invited?"

"No one would dare entertain without inviting the Harrisons. They're the first family of Piedmont Point."

I dreaded asking the next question. "Do they invite the children, too?"

"Not the young ones, but occasionally the teenagers come if they have nothing better to do."

I felt as if I were sinking in quicksand. Suppose Blake came to the party? He'd find out about me! I'd have to make sure he didn't show up!

Rose Marie chuckled. "I know you're hoping young Blake will come. Sweetie, Mrs. Beaumont's opinion of you would jump ten points if she thought one of the Harrison boys was interested in you."

"Don't tell her, please!" Now I had something to worry about all weekend.

"Why?" Rose Marie asked.

"You heard her say she didn't hire me to meet boys."

"Not just any boy. But a Harrison — she'd throw all the rules out the window."

"Are Mrs. Harrison and Mrs. Beaumont good friends?" I asked.

"Oh, they serve on committees together and occasionally they see each other socially. They're not bosom buddies, if that's what you mean. The Harrisons are in a class by themselves — socially, politically, and financially."

I wasn't hungry anymore. What could I do to keep Blake away from the party?

I took the boys upstairs for their naps and packed my overnight bag for my trip home. There was just no easy way out of the trouble I'd gotten myself into.

My bus was due to leave at eight o'clock that evening, and after dinner Mrs. Beaumont said her husband would like to talk to me in his study. Here it comes, I thought. I felt just like I was being sent to the principal's office — only Mr. Beaumont was wearing white shorts and a Lacoste sport shirt. He was bald and wore what hair remained in a styled fringe over his ears.

He looked uncomfortable and I didn't know why. As vice-president of a giant company, he was probably used to firing people by the dozen. He tapped his pipe several times against his desk. "Shannon, Mrs. Beaumont asked me to speak to you about the incident today."

"I'm very sorry, Mr. Beaumont. I . . ."

He held up his hand. "Please, I know all the details. The story hour was excused early and you were having a Coke with a boy you met at the pier."

I flushed. "It was Ryan Webster. I've known him all summer."

"I'm acquainted with the family. Mr. Webster services our boats. The important fact is Scott walked home unattended. People in our position are always concerned with security."

He made me sound like an irresponsible fool, and I felt the tears well up in my eyes and threaten to spill over.

His voice softened. "I'm sure you won't let it happen again now that you realize how serious the consequences could be. On the whole, Shannon, we have been very pleased with your work and the boys are fond of you. We have considered asking you to return to Boston with us in September and continue your care of the boys. You could attend school there."

"Oh, but I couldn't do that! This is my senior year!" I exclaimed.

"We have fine schools in Boston."

"I'm sure you do. But I want to graduate with my friends. I've known most of my classmates since kindergarten."

"I do understand, Shannon, but please consider the offer. You may change your mind."

Did he really think I wanted to make a career of baby-sitting? I wondered. I was all the more determined to further my education and enter a profession.

My dad met me at the bus station in the old Pinto that had been our second car. Now it was the family car since we had had to sell our newer Mercury when my dad lost his job. He looked older, somehow, with deep-seated lines of fatigue in his face, but his smile was the same.

"Hello, honey. How is the job going?" he asked as I slid into the seat beside him.

"Not bad. I spend a lot of time on the beach and they have a great cook."

"Are the Beaumonts good employers? Are they considerate of you?"

"It's a job, Dad, but I'm not going to make it my life's work."

"I should hope not," he smiled.

"How are things going with you?"

"I'm still an unemployment statistic. I've about exhausted the job possibilities in the area and I've begun to send some resumes further afield. I have an interview in New London next week. It's the first promising lead I've had in months."

"New London, Connecticut?" I asked.

"Right."

"But that's out of state. How would Mom feel about moving?"

"She's expressing her opinions quite emphatically. She's dead set against moving and she said it wouldn't be fair to have you change schools your senior year."

I sat quietly. Maybe I wouldn't graduate with my class after all. This was another worry to tuck away in that corner of my already troubled mind.

Dad stopped for a red light. "I'm sure your mother would change her mind if I get the position. It's often difficult for a forty-five-year-old man to find a new job and we could lose everything if I don't find substantial employment soon."

"I just got paid, Dad. You're welcome to the money if you need it."

He gave a wry smile. "Thanks, Shannon, but we're not that desperate. You use the money to buy your school clothes. That will be a big help. I worry about the future — whether you and Ben can go to college."

"If Ben and I want an education, we'll get it. There are scholarships and student loans and jobs on campus if we want to work. We'll make out all right."

We drove along in silence. I knew my father was a proud man and it hurt his pride not to be able to provide well for his family. I hoped he would get the job in Connecticut, even if it meant we had to move.

Mom wanted to know all about my job — how the Beaumonts lived, how many servants they had, if they entertained often. It wasn't until Dad went to bed and we were watching a late rerun on TV that she spoke about what was troubling her.

"You don't know what it's been like these past few weeks, Shannon," she said wearily. "Your Uncle Allen and Aunt Gladys and the two children were here last weekend from California and your father wouldn't let on he was out of work. He insisted we show them as good a time as they showed us when we visited there last year. We took them all over and Saturday night we went to the King James, that fancy new restaurant, and the bill came to over a hundred dollars. I could

46

have outfitted Ben for school with that money."

"Dad and Uncle Allen were always competitive," I said to my mother. "Dad has his pride and you really can't blame him."

My mother sighed. "We're getting behind in our bills and I don't know how we're going to pay the heating bills this winter. I could go back to teaching but your father is so macho and behind the times he doesn't want his wife to work!"

"Maybe he'll get the job in Connecticut," I offered.

"That's another thing. I told him I won't move and that's final."

I went to bed feeling depressed. My parents' problems, the situation I had gotten myself into with Blake, the fact I might be changing schools — they all spun around in my head like a kaleidoscope pattern in gloomy colors. This really was a messed-up summer.

My brother Ben arrived home from Scout camp Saturday afternoon looking tanned and healthy from his two-week stay. He had gifts he'd made for all of us: a hammered copper bracelet for me, a tooled leather wallet for my dad, and a wooden tray for my mother. He'd had a great time and talked nonstop about the badges he'd earned, the water sports, and the tricks they played on the counselors — like putting itching powder in their beds.

I felt good seeing him so happy and knowing I had had a small part in it. Ben's asthma had cheated him out of so many things most kids took for granted.

I slept late Sunday morning. In the afternoon Ben and I walked down to Abbott's for a frozen custard. I chose blueberry and Ben settled for peach and we sat down on one of the benches to eat our cones.

Ben looked troubled. "Do you think Mom and Dad will get a divorce? They fight all the time and Mom says if Dad gets that job in Connecticut he'll go there alone."

"Don't worry, Ben. Mom rants and raves a lot but in the end she usually sees things Dad's way. They fight because they're uptight and worried."

"I don't know what I'd do if they got a divorce. Moving doesn't even bother me. I'd miss my friends — but they could move away from here, too."

"You've got a point. People move all the time," I agreed.

"Besides, I like new experiences. There's a submarine base in New London. Wouldn't it be neat to watch the subs maneuver?"

"A nice pastime on a slow day," I replied. We concentrated on our cones for a while.

"Did you make any friends on the Cape?" Ben asked.

"I met two boys. You'd like them both. Blake has a sailboat and Ryan pilots a tour boat for his uncle."

"That's neat. I wish I could visit you there." Ben wiped his hands on his pants.

"Just between you and me, Mrs. Beaumont

can be pretty grim. I'm sure she wouldn't approve of my bringing guests."

I finished my cone and we walked home. It would soon be time for me to board the bus for my return trip. I wondered what the week ahead of me would bring.

I had only been away from here for a month, but now I noticed how shabby the storefronts looked along Main Street. The vacant stores looked desolate and abandoned. I seemed to be seeing things through Blake's eyes. Even the Crossroads, the high school hangout, which had seemed so right, now looked tacky, with white tape zigzagging across the crack in the plate-glass window and posters advertising the Labor Day Fish Derby and the Roast Pork Supper at the Methodist Church. The hanging plants in the window — the Swedish ivy and the Wandering Jew — looked faded and yellow, as if they had hung in the sun too long.

As we turned down our street I became aware that our house needed painting and the lawn looked patchy. I had never noticed it before.

Had I changed? I didn't think so. I just kept wondering how my home and my town would look to Blake. I couldn't keep him away from here forever. Someday, I would have to bring him here to meet my parents.

CHAPTER FIVE _____

Now I know why people write to Ann Landers for advice when they get themselves into a no-win situation. They don't know where to turn, and Ann Landers is available to everyone right in the daily newspapers. All you need is the price of a postage stamp.

I knew what she would say if I ever wrote to her. She never minces words. She would reply, "Level with the guy and take your lumps! You deserve it!"

All the way back to Piedmont Point I thought about Blake and what a disaster it would be if he decided to come to the party. I found myself wishing I were ten years old again, and my biggest problem was how to get rid of the excess snails in my fish tank without disturbing the plant life. I wasn't really a deceitful person. My biggest personality fault was that I was hung up on trying to please people and being the person they expected me to be. This time, I had tried too hard.

At first, I thought I was pleasing Blake by pretending to be a girl from his affluent world. But I had been wrong. Terribly wrong.

At the Beaumonts' on Wednesday, everything was geared toward that night's party. The draperies came back from the cleaners and were hung at the windows. Someone came in and shampooed the rugs. An extra cleaning lady was hired to shine the silver and wash the windows.

Mrs. Beaumont kept moaning about how difficult it was to entertain in the summer home. "We're really just roughing it here on the Cape," she explained. "My good china is back in Boston, but I didn't want to risk bringing it here just for the party."

I smiled to myself. She didn't know what roughing it was. She should go camping with my family at Loon Lake. I wanted to ask her if the Harrisons were coming to the party but I didn't quite dare. I was sure luck was with me. I hadn't seen Blake since I'd come back. Maybe he had called Friday to tell me he would be away for a few days. I hoped he would stay away until after the party.

The caterer arrived to talk over last-minute arrangements with Mrs. Beaumont, and I wandered out into the kitchen to see Rose Marie. She had been sulking for the past few days as preparations were being made for the party.

"Will you look at this menu!" she said disdainfully. "Beef Wellington! That's no big deal. I was fixing that when the caterer was still in diapers. And mousseline sauce over broccoli! Why, that's nothing but egg yolks and cream and lemon juice."

I sat down on a kitchen stool and helped myself to a piece of celery. "I'll take your cooking any day, Rose Marie. In fact, my mother would like the recipes for some of your dishes. I was raving about them all last weekend."

Rose Marie brightened. "Would she? You just let me know which ones and I'll write them down."

Mrs. Beaumont stopped me as I was going upstairs to see if Scott and Robbie had awakened from their naps. "Shannon, when you first came here to work, I told you your evenings would be free when we were at home. However, this is a large party and if the boys awaken and came downstairs, I won't be able to leave my guests and attend to them. Would you mind staying in tonight and looking after them?"

"No, of course not, Mrs. Beaumont," I answered. "I haven't any plans."

"Good, I knew I could depend on you. If the boys are awake, why don't you take them on the beach for a while and get them out from underfoot? I hope they will be tired enough to sleep soundly tonight."

I went upstairs. Long ago Robbie had learned to lower the sides of his crib. He had climbed out and was sitting on the oval braided rug playing with his Planet Destroyer set.

"Play, Sha-na-na," he invited. I sat down on the floor and we catapulted foam missiles at each other and at Scott who was still sleeping. Robbie's shrieks when he scored a direct hit finally awakened Scott, so I dressed the boys and we went downstairs.

The florist arrived with beautiful flower arrangements for the tables. The rooms looked like pictures in a magazine.

I took the boys across the road to the beach. Jamie was sitting on the sand with a boy and she called, "Shannon, over here!"

I settled the boys down in the sand with their bulldozer and dump trucks before I joined Jamie and her friend. "Where are the little girls?" I asked. "Aren't you baby-sitting?"

"The Kingsleys are in Vermont and I have the week to myself. Shannon, this is my boyfriend, Mac." Mac had brown eyes and reddish hair. He was starting to grow a beard that was at the unkempt stage.

"Hi, Shannon," he smiled. "You're a nice addition to the beach. Are you staying at the Beaumonts'?"

"That's me," I replied.

"We're painting the Harrisons' house and Blake told me he had met a girl who was a guest of the Beaumonts' for the summer."

"Not a guest!" Jamie said. "Are you sure you heard right, Mac?"

"That's what the man said."

I must have looked stricken, for Jamie said quickly, "Is something wrong, Shannon?"

I would have to tell them and that would make three people who would know about my lies. Ryan, Jamie, and Mac. With three people knowing, it wouldn't remain a secret much longer.

The words stuck in my throat, reluctant to be spoken. Then they tumbled out. "Blake doesn't know I'm the baby-sitter. He thinks I'm a guest."

Jamie looked surprised. "Why would you tell him a stupid thing like that?"

"At first it was just a joke."

She was concerned. "And now you're falling in love with him?"

I nodded miserably.

Mac had a big grin on his face. He spoke in a high falsetto voice. "Blake, darling, I'm not the rich jet-setter you think I am, but just a lil' old Cinderella-type baby-sitter!"

"Shut up, Mac!" Jamie demanded. "You have a sick sense of humor!"

"I think it's hilarious," Mac continued. "You're making a fool of Blake in front of his friends. I'd like to be around when he finds out!"

I bowed my head. The last thing in the world I wanted to do was hurt Blake.

"Mac, you're just jealous of Blake," Jamie said. "It's not his fault he's wealthy. It doesn't make him a bad person."

"I didn't say he was. It just serves him

right for being able to drive a Porsche. It evens things out a bit. I'm going to buy a Coke. Would you girls like one?"

I shook my head. "Make mine organic apple juice if they have it," Jamie said. When we were alone she faced me. "I'm sorry, Shannon. Maybe it will turn out all right."

"What do you think? Will he be really angry?"

Jamie traced her initials in the sand. "Blake's never dated any town girls. It's always been girls here for the summer from Boston and New York and places like that. I know he has a lot of pride. He wouldn't want people laughing at him."

I looked away, feeling so wretched I could die.

"He seems to care about you, Shannon. Is there a boy back home?"

"Our town is small and everyone expects you to pair off. I went steady with a boy this spring. He was gung-ho on cars, and when we dated I had the feeling he'd rather be tearing down the transmission on his car or installing brake linings."

"I know the type. We have them here, too."

"We finally drifted apart because we had nothing in common. I felt we were both wasting our time."

"No regrets?" Jamie asked.

"None whatsoever," I replied. "When he kissed me, it was like my little brother Ben kissing me good night. It's different with

Blake. I want him to touch me and kiss me and hold me."

Jamie let the sand drift through her fingers. "I know what you mean. Some people think I'm fast because of the tattoo and the rough way I talk sometimes, but it's been only Mac since the seventh grade. I can't imagine life without him. It would be like cutting me in two."

We were both silent for a while. Robbie and Scott played quietly with their trucks and the only sound was the pounding of the surf.

Mac came back with the apple juice. "I've got to pick up my brother at work, Jamie. Want to ride along?"

"I will if you'll stop at the cleaner's so I can pick up my blazer. The label says wash and wear but I didn't want to take a chance washing it. So long, Shannon. Try not to worry."

"Nice to have met you, Shannon," Mac remarked. "Anyone who can put one over on a Harrison gets my vote. You've made my day."

"Leave her alone, bully," Jamie replied.

After they left I went over and played in the sand with the boys. We built roads and excavated for swimming pools, canals, and housing projects with the bulldozer.

I heard my name called and I looked up to see Blake jogging toward me. I felt a curious mixture of pleasure and apprehension — pleasure at seeing him and apprehension at being forced to connive and lie again. He dropped to his knees on the sand, caught my arms, and kissed me. I felt such a rush of feeling it left me glowing.

"I've missed you so," he said softly. "I couldn't wait to get back."

"I've missed you, too. Rose Marie said you called on Friday."

"I called to tell you my brother and I decided to visit friends camping in the Catskills. It was a dumb idea and I was ready to come home Sunday. How was your trip home?"

"Uneventful," I answered.

"Are you still keeping your address a secret?"

"I told you you wouldn't recognize the town."

Blake smiled. "Don't you realize I could find out by asking Mrs. Beaumont tonight?"

"Tonight?" I knew what he meant but I was stalling for time.

"When I got home today I saw the invitation to the Beaumonts' party tonight, on my mother's desk."

I could feel the hard, steady pounding of my heart as adrenaline pulsed through my body in fight-or-flight readiness. With the quick response of a guilty conscience I replied, "You don't want to go to their boring old party. They'll probably be dancing to taped-in Lawrence Welk music."

"Just a minute, love. The Heritage House is catering the food and that's enough to interest me. My parents always have them for their parties."

"All boys ever think about is food!" I said as I tried to think of more excuses for Blake not to attend the party.

My hand was buried in his. "That's not true. Most of the time I think of you."

I *had* to keep him away. "The party is for middle-aged people. We don't want to hang around them."

"Okay. We'll eat and then go to a movie. Any special one you'd like to see?"

Panic beat at me. I couldn't leave the house. I had to watch the children. "No, I don't want to see a movie!"

He frowned. "You don't want to see a movie and you don't want me to come to the party." Hurt crept into his voice. "If you would rather not see me, I'll make other plans."

No matter what I did I'd lose him. I was so tired of making up lies. I turned away under his steady gaze. "I can't figure you out, Shannon," he said quietly. "You're like two different people — loving and outgoing one minute and withdrawn and secretive the next. If you have a problem, can't we talk it over? Is there someone back home and you feel guilty about dating me?"

"No," I said quickly. "There's no one else."

"What is it then? Is it something I've done?"

"It's not that." I struggled to keep from crying. I wanted to blurt out the truth but then I'd risk losing him.

He turned me around so I had to face him. "I think there is someone else. Is it Ryan?"

"Ryan? I haven't seen him all week."

Blake's look was questioning. "But you do like him?"

"Yes, I like him, but only as a friend. Is this an inquisition?"

"I'm just trying to understand why you don't want me at the party tonight."

"You'll be bored," I answered.

"Just the same, I'm going to stop by. It'll be fun. We might get a few laughs." He gave me a quick kiss. "I'll see you around nine."

I sat in my room in my best lacy underwear for a long time, dreading my next move. The mirror reflected how scared I felt. I would have to dress and go downstairs and pretend to Blake I was a guest at the party. I'd have to try and stay out of Mrs. Beaumont's way, too, and I didn't know how I was going to manage that. If Blake found me out tonight, I hoped he loved me enough to forgive me.

I had no idea what people wore to parties at Piedmont Point. I had brought one dress with me from home in case Blake ever took me any place where a dress was more appropriate than jeans. Finally I walked around to the other side of the bed where I had laid out my dress and picked it up. The dress was beige with a brown woven belt; I had bought it in April when I represented the school on the debate team competing at Hartford.

59

The least I could do was try to look my best tonight, if it was to be our last night together. I wanted to wear my hair up in a French braid. I had seen the style in a women's magazine. I brushed my hair on top of my head. Then I carefully made the braid and pinned it up. By the time I'd finished, my arms ached. I thought the style made me look at least nineteen.

I slipped the dress over my head and tied my belt with shaky fingers. How could I ever watch for Blake and avoid Mrs. Beaumont?

I looked in on the children and they were both asleep. I breathed a prayer they would stay asleep for the duration of the party. They had fallen asleep quickly this evening. I had read them two bedtime stories instead of the usual one, but Robbie had fallen asleep before I'd gotten to the last page.

I walked down the hall and peered over the banister at the party below. People were everywhere and uniformed maids moved among the guests with drinks and trays of hors d'oeuvres. At the far end of the room couples were dancing to the music of a four-piece jazz combo. The music, the talking, and the laughter made a pleasant party din that floated up to where I stood.

I was surprised to see a few young people gathered in little groups. They all seemed so sure of themselves; they were probably discussing all the exciting things they were doing this summer. I sat down in the shadow of some huge plants that had been brought in for the occasion. I felt miserable and inferior; I had no business being at Piedmont Point. It had brought me nothing but heartbreak.

Then I saw Blake coming in the door with an older couple I presumed were his parents. He was wearing a blue blazer and white flannels; he looked gorgeous. He paused in the doorway and looked around, and I knew I couldn't hide much longer. I stood up and started down the stairs.

CHAPTER SIX

Blake saw me and crossed the room. "You look terrific, Shannon. Really sensational. Until tonight I've never seen you wear a dress."

"Is the dress an improvement?"

He smiled with a special intimacy. "You always look great." He glanced around the room. "I thought Ryan might be here."

"He wasn't invited."

"I still don't know why you didn't want me to come tonight."

"I'm not a party person." I hated myself. It was all so awful having to lie to Blake.

"I find that hard to believe." He looked around. "I've been out on the boat and I'm starved. I hope they haven't eaten yet."

I looked nervously over my shoulder for Mrs. Beaumont. "No, I think they're serving at ten o'clock. Would you like to dance?" Out on the terrace Mrs. Beaumont wasn't as likely to spot me.

"Let's circulate around and see who's here. I'd like you to meet my parents."

I was dismayed. "Oh, no! Not tonight!" His parents were certain to ask questions!

He took my arm. "What do you mean? You look beautiful."

"Please, not now, Blake!"

In spite of my protests he led me across the room to where his parents were admiring a painting over the mantel. They looked just as I'd expected they would. Even if they had been wearing warm-up suits, you would have known they were wealthy socialites.

"Mother and Dad, I would like you to meet Shannon McCabe."

Blake's mother was a tall, regal blonde in a pale blue gown with a sapphire pendant at her throat. Mr. Harrison looked distinguished, with graying sideburns and a deep tan he'd probably acquired sailing on his yacht or playing golf.

"Hello, Shannon," Mrs. Harrison said. "So you are the young lady who is visiting the Beaumonts this summer."

I stood there like a robot trying to smile — and you know how hard it is for robots to smile. I must have looked ghastly.

Mr. Harrison said pleasantly, "You must be the reason Blake cut short his Catskill trip. I can't say that I blame him."

"Are you enjoying your vacation on the Cape?" Blake's mother asked.

Blake answered, "She is since she met me."

His father placed a hand on Blake's shoulder. "Then we may see more of you this summer, son. Why don't you bring Shannon over to brunch on Sunday. You young people might like to go to the races at Edgartown with us."

"We may have other plans, Dad. I thought Shannon and I might take a ride up to Provincetown. She's never been there."

Another crisis! I had to work this weekend!

"You've never been to Provincetown!" Mr Harrison exclaimed. "Where are you from, my dear?"

I glanced furtively at Blake. He put an arm around me. "She's from a little town you never heard of."

Mrs. Harrison looked puzzled as Blake led me away. I breathed a small sigh of relief. I had gotten over *that* hurdle. Then I realized I hadn't spoken one word. What a dummy they must have thought I was! We circled the room, Blake stopping occasionally to greet friends while I tried to make myself as inconspicuous as possible.

The musicians were trying to please everybody and the numbers they played ranged from golden oldies like "Stardust" and "Smoke Gets in Your Eyes" to soft rock for the over thirty-fives who pretended they were still sixteen. They looked sort of silly twisting and jerking about. I hoped I would age gracefully.

Then I spotted Mrs. Beaumont in a flowing India-print dress, moving among the guests, laughing and talking vivaciously. She was heading in my direction and suddenly our eyes met. Her eyes widened in astonishment and mine looked frantically for an escape.

Should I take one of the trays from the maids and pretend I was helping to serve the refreshments? To my relief Mrs. Beaumont was hailed by a couple holding drinks who demanded her attention. I slipped out the French doors and onto the flagstone terrace leaving Blake talking to his friends.

He would think I was impolite, but it was better than having Mrs. Beaumont collar me in front of him to ask me what I was doing at her party.

I waited in the shadows, watching the doors, but it was Blake instead of Mrs. Beaumont who strode through them. He looked annoyed. "Why did you run out on me? I planned to introduce you to my friends. I'm going to room with Jerome Northrop at college this fall and I wanted to show you off."

"It was so warm in there," I answered lamely. I expected Mrs. Beaumont to burst through the French doors any minute.

"Shannon, what's happening between us? We hit it off so well in the beginning and now we seem to be growing apart."

"I'm sorry. It was rude of me. Would you like to see the rest of the house? There's a billiard table down in the family room and you might like to shoot some pool."

"Don't try to change the subject. I don't want to see the house and I don't want to shoot pool. What's going on?"

"Don't ask questions, Blake. Can't we just *be*?"

"This mysterious attitude of yours bugs me. I can't take much more of it."

I put my arms around him and laid my head on his shoulder. "Just take me as I am."

He kissed the top of my head. "I don't understand you, Shannon. But I really care for you."

We walked through the flower-scented garden and down to the dock. I took off my heels and walked barefoot on the sand that still held some of the warmth of the afternoon sun. The lush loveliness of the night was something I would always remember. A huge orange moon hung over the water and the stars looked so close it didn't seem possible they were millions of light-years away.

Blake pointed out the constellations Great Bear, Pegasus, and Hercules. The only sound was the creaking of a boat against its mooring. As I was looking up at the stars he kissed me. Soon his kisses were so intense they frightened me, for my body seemed to have a will of its own.

"What are we going to do about each other?" he asked as I drew myself away. "I'll be leaving for college in a few weeks."

He'll know all about me by then, I thought sadly, and it will be all over between us.

"Will you come up to college on weekends?" he asked.

"To stay with you? You don't know my mother. She would disown me."

"When am I going to meet your parents?"

"Someday," I promised.

"Let's head back—they must be serving dinner by now. I'm really hungry," Blake said. We walked back to the house with our arms locked around each other. I'd have to try and avoid Mrs. Beaumont again. I hoped Scott and Robbie hadn't awakened again and joined the party. If they had, I would just run away. I'd hitchhike back home and stay there.

A line had formed for the buffet and the maids were serving the guests a food extravaganza that looked like an advertisement for Swedish cuisine on an ocean liner. "Wow!" Blake exclaimed as he handed me a plate and happily began filling his own.

I placed a few dabs of food on my plate, terribly nervous about Mrs. Beaumont. I had just reached the avocado mousse when I felt a firm hand on my arm. "May I see you for a moment, Shannon?" Mrs. Beaumont's glare was as icy as a snow cone.

She led me into Mr. Beaumont's study and partially closed the door. Her voice was pointed, significant. "Shannon, I know you are not experienced in working as part of a household staff, but when we give a formal party it is for invited guests only. The help does not mingle with the guests socially. Your common sense should have told you that."

"I'm sorry . . ."

"You're always sorry when it's too late.

You came to me with excellent references from Miss Linn, your guidance counselor. She said that you were intelligent, responsible, and a school leader. You have disappointed me now on several occasions. Did you know that Robbie came downstairs in his pajamas a half-hour ago?"

"Oh, no!"

"Yes. I had to awaken Rose Marie to attend to him." Through the half-opened door she saw Blake waiting impatiently for me with his plate of food. "Where did you meet Blake Harrison?"

"On the beach."

"How long have you known him?"

"About a week," I answered.

She looked down at the plate I was carrying that held a few carrot sticks and some creamed chicken. Her voice softened slightly. "You may eat with Blake, but as soon as you're finished I want you to go upstairs and stay with the children. Is that perfectly clear?"

"Yes, Mrs. Beaumont." I hurried from the study.

"What was that all about?" Blake demanded when I joined him.

"Nothing important."

"Was she picking on you again?"

"Not really." At least Mrs. Beaumont had the decency this time not to shame me in front of Blake.

"She was probably roping you into taking care of her kids tomorrow. I think you're too

68

accommodating and she takes advantage of you." He glanced over at the table. "Do you want to get back in the serving line again?"

"No, I have enough."

"Where can we sit down?"

"There's a little table out on the terrace if it's not taken," I said. I led him outside to the stone table with the circular bench and we sat down. I hoped he didn't notice that my hands were shaking. It had been a close call.

Blake buttered a roll. "You saw me talking with Jerome. We've decided to go to Boston tomorrow and look things over on campus."

Tomorrow was my day off. I could have spent all day with Blake.

He must have seen my disappointment, for he reached over and took my hand. "I'm planning to spend every moment of the weekend with you. Don't make any other plans."

Couldn't anything turn out right? I had to work this weekend.

"If Mrs. Beaumont wants you to watch the kids this weekend, tell her to get a baby-sitter."

My mind raced frantically, digging for an excuse, but I couldn't come up with one. I pushed the creamed chicken around on my plate, pretending I was eating. I'd barely escaped exposure tonight, only to face another predicament this weekend.

"I would have liked you to meet Jerome and his girl friend Gina, but they've left now," Blake said. "Jerome is one of my oldest friends. We both went to Deerfield Academy and last summer we traveled through Europe with our class. Have you ever been to Europe?"

That was a laugh. "No," I answered.

"You would have liked France. This is the last summer I'll just bum around. I want to get a job on a newspaper next summer to gain some experience. Jerome's father publishes a paper in Connecticut and he might find me a spot. Are you coming to the Cape next summer, Shannon?"

"No, I want to do something with photography. I'd work for nothing to get experience in one of the fields."

We had finished eating and I knew I couldn't stay much longer. Blake solved that problem when he said he was going to leave, as Jerome and he were getting an early start in the morning for Boston. He kissed me good night and reminded me about the weekend we were going to spend together.

After he left I went upstairs and checked on the boys. They were sleeping soundly. Poo Dog had fallen on the floor and I picked him up and placed him beside Robbie. He would look for him the first thing in the morning when he awoke.

I undressed and showered, letting the hot water ease the little knots of tension that had built up during the party. But when I got into bed, sleep wouldn't come.

You should be warned about falling in love for the first time, I thought. It can be too painful.

CHAPTER SEVEN _____

Thursday was my day off and the day stretched before me without plans. With Blake in Boston I wouldn't have to juggle my lies — but I missed him. I hated sharing him with anyone because we had too little time left to be together. A hundred times I had prepared what I would say to him when I told him the truth about myself, but the time never seemed right.

I could take the bus today to the shopping mall and shop around for school clothes, but with the temperature in the high eighties I wasn't in the mood for trying on sweaters and wool skirts. It was a day for being outdoors in the sun.

Ryan had convinced me that there was an active market for outdoor photography and that the Cape was a natural subject. Tour companies, travel agencies, airlines, hotels, and tourist bureaus had a continuing need for promotion photos. I had hoped to bring back a portfolio of great pictures to impress my guidance counselor. It might even help toward a scholarship.

I wondered if Ryan would like to join me today. I hadn't seen him since the story-hour episode at the library and I was sure Mrs. Beaumont had scared him off. I felt guilty that I hadn't called and convinced him it wasn't his fault, but then my head wasn't on straight since I'd met Blake.

I looked up Ryan's number and dialed. A child answered the phone. Ryan had told me he had a little sister. "This is Shannon," I said. "Is Ryan at home?"

"He's mowing the lawn. I'll call him for you."

He seemed glad I had called. "I thought you were angry with me, Shannon. Mrs. Beaumont really nailed you to the wall. Is she always like that?"

"I can't blame her for being angry, but I didn't like her involving you," I answered.

"I stayed away because I didn't want to make any more trouble for you."

"I don't think she wants to prevent me from having friends. She just wants to make sure I do my job," I said.

"Isn't today your day off? How are you spending it?"

"I'd like to roam around and take some pictures. Want to join me? I could pack a picnic lunch."

"I have to work, Shannon. A senior citizen group has chartered the tour boat for a day trip. Would you like to go along?"

I hesitated. I really wanted to shoot pictures today.

"You can sit up front and keep me company. Bring your camera. We'll be stopping at some historical Indian and Pilgrim sites, and there're always the picturesque harbors along the way."

"Okay. You talked me into it," I agreed.

"I'll be glad to have you along. Some of the senior citizens could use some assistance."

"Sure, I'll help. I like senior citizens. My grandmother was one of the best friends I had."

"Good. Meet me down at the pier by ten-fifteen and don't forget to bring your camera. I'll bring mine, too."

Scott and Robbie came into my room as I finished dressing. "Where are you going, Shannon?" Scott asked.

"I'm going on a boat trip with some elderly people."

"Like my grandpa and grandma?"

"No, they're even older than your grandparents. We're going on Ryan's boat."

"Frisbee!" Robbie exclaimed.

"Perhaps Ryan will play Frisbee with you tomorrow. I'll ask him," I promised.

"I haven't seen Ryan all week," Scott remarked. "Is Blake your boyfriend now?"

"Ryan thought he got me into trouble the day you walked home alone from the story hour."

"I got home all right," Scott said.

"I know you did but you gave us all a scare."

"Did you know Robbie went downstairs to the party last night?" Scott said.

Sighing, I picked up my camera. "I certainly do."

"Rose Marie was mad my mom waked her up to take care of Robbie. He wanted to stay at the party and he cried a lot when she brought him upstairs."

"I'll have to apologize to her," I said. I dreaded facing her. Rose Marie let you know exactly what she thought of you.

The boys wandered off and I went downstairs to the kitchen. "Good morning," I said timidly, waiting at the door.

Rose Marie slammed my orange juice down on the table. "Well, miss, I hope you don't expect Mrs. Beaumont to give you a good reference if you ever want a babysitting job again on the Cape. You seem to get into trouble every time you turn around."

I sat down at the table. "I'm sorry, Rose Marie."

"I was hired as a cook, not a baby-sitter. I wasn't good enough to cook for the party last night, but it's all right to wake me up to do your job."

I made circles on the table with my orange juice glass. Should I confess to Rose Marie? I decided against it. Too many people knew already that I was a phony. Instead, I said, "I want to make it up to you. I'll help you with the dishes every night this week."

"That's no big deal. We have a dishwasher."

"When is your day off?" I asked.

"Tuesday."

"I'll take you to a movie," I suggested.

"I can see a movie every night on TV," she said stubbornly.

"Then let me buy you a present. I feel badly that you had to get up and care for Robbie."

"Ain't necessary to buy me no present," she replied. "Just don't let it happen again."

"I'm going to buy you one just the same." Rose Marie didn't spend much money on herself and I thought a summer purse would make a nice gift.

She poured herself a cup of coffee and sat down at the table with me. "If it had been any boy other than Blake Harrison last night, you wouldn't have gotten off so easily. Mrs. Beaumont can't understand what he sees in you, with all the classy summer girls at Piedmont Point."

I grinned. "He likes me for my money."

"I'll just bet he does," she chuckled. Then, more seriously, she said, "I've seen a lot of summer romances fade away. Just don't let him break your heart, honey."

I really wanted to tell her the truth but I didn't dare. Suppose she told Mrs. Beaumont? Rose Marie was gruff and she talked to me like an aunt, but she had been good to me, too. I did think a lot of her and she might even understand. But it was too big a risk to take.

She stirred her coffee. "Where did you get

the nerve to invite yourself to the party? Haven't you any sense at all, girl? We're not supposed to hobnob with society at their parties." She chuckled again. "I would have liked to see Mrs. Beaumont's face when she saw you all dressed up and sashaying among her highfalutin friends."

"Her mouth just sort of sagged. It was quite something," I said. Then I took my dishes over to the sink.

"Today's your day off, isn't it? What are you doing?"

"I'm spending the day on the tour boat with Ryan Webster."

"Another one? No wonder Mrs. Beaumont thinks you're boy-crazy."

Down at the pier a yellow minibus was discharging its passengers and I went over to help Ryan. The senior citizens all wore large name tags pinned to their shirts or dresses. At least a dozen relied on canes, and two ladies used walkers to move slowly across the dock. Others moved briskly, proud of their mobility and independence.

CORA MILLER, read the name tag of a tiny, white-haired lady who fussed over the other passengers like a mother hen, assisting those who walked with difficulty, assigning seats on the boat, retrieving sweaters and shawls left in the bus. She wore a denim wrap-around skirt and a T-shirt with the words GOLDEN-AGE SWINGERS across the front.

I counted only three men in the group. One cantankerous senior citizen, puffing on a cigar, made his presence known as he shuffled along with a cane. He complained to Cora, "I could have stayed back at the Center and played euchre but you had to drag me along."

"Hush, Clement Hooper," Cora said. "You know you will enjoy the outing once we're underway. You spend entirely too much time playing cards. The fresh salt air will do you good."

"I've been inhaling salt air for eighty-one years and a boat trip ain't no treat for me. When I was a kid I piloted a ferry between the mainland and Martha's Vineyard."

"Now, don't go wandering down memory lane, Clement," Cora admonished. "We have to live for today. Just get in the boat and make up your mind to enjoy the trip."

When Clement was seated in the boat, Cora came over to me. "You must be Shannon," she said. "Ryan told me you would be coming along and I'm grateful for your help. I'm supposed to be in charge but I have my hands full. A lot of my friends here tell me they've never been on a boat before."

"I'm glad to help out."

"I'm terrified of the water," Cora confessed. "Get me ten feet offshore and I'm rigid with fear."

"Then I admire you for coming along today. The others seem to depend on you," I answered.

"I have my good health and I like to help those who aren't so fortunate."

Ryan came over and put his arm around me. "Cora, have you met Shannon?"

"We've just introduced ourselves, Ryan." Cora lowered her voice. "Are you sure we won't run into bad weather?"

"The marine broadcast promised perfect weather conditions," he reassured her.

Her voice was anxious. "I hope we get home before dark."

"We'll be docking about eight o'clock," Ryan replied.

Cora raised doubts in my mind and I looked at the *Treasure Island* skeptically, remembering how Blake had made fun of it that first day on the beach. The boat was old but it appeared to be in good condition. The mahogany hull gleamed softly in the sunlight.

When everyone was seated in the boat, Ryan gave a brief speech explaining that he would announce points of interest along the way. Various stops would be made for sightseeing and those who wished could go ashore. I took the seat up front next to Ryan and readied my camera for any interesting subjects I might encounter.

Once we got underway, everyone seemed to relax. We stayed close to shore and over the loudspeaker, Ryan pointed out the gull colonies on the dunes and the cranberry bogs.

Cora led the group in singing songs like "Peg of My Heart" and "Put on Your Old Gray Bonnet." The voices floated out over the water and people in passing boats smiled and waved. I took pictures of the group and promised to send copies to the Senior Citizen Center.

At noon we ate at Old Harbor Inn and later, while our passengers browsed through the adjoining souvenir shop, Ryan and I took a walk along the beach. He took my hand. "You don't know how happy you made me, coming along today. I wish you could be beside me always."

"I like being with you," I replied. "I feel relaxed and comfortable."

He smiled ruefully. "Comfortable, like an old shoe?"

"Of course not. We're good friends. Do you know what my grandmother's definition of a friend was?"

"I can't imagine," Ryan replied.

"A friend is someone who knows all about you but still likes you."

"That's neat — but I want to be more than a friend," he said obstinately.

"We share an interest in photography," I offered.

"That's not what I mean and you know it. If Blake hadn't shown up on the beach that day, you and I would have shared a great summer."

We walked in silence for a while and I wondered why it was so hard for a boy and a girl to be just friends. I hated to hurt people but I was hurting Ryan, and before the summer was over, maybe I would hurt Blake, too.

"Everyone is pairing off this summer, but all I think about is you," Ryan said.

It would be wrong for me to encourage him, to let him think he had a chance. I knew how he felt. All I could think about was Blake.

"Ryan, you've only known me a few weeks. How do you know I'm the right person for you?"

"You don't understand," he said quietly. "You don't understand at all."

Our departure from the restaurant's dock was delayed for nearly a half-hour when we couldn't find Clement. Ryan finally located him in a nearby bar where he was having a beer, and Cora scolded him when we brought him back to the boat.

"Nobody on this tour I can talk to," he complained. "There're only two other men and they're both deaf!"

"Well, I'm not deaf," Cora replied. "You can sit and talk to me."

"I think there's a little romance going on," one of the ladies whispered, "but neither one will admit it."

When everyone was seated in the boat, Ryan had trouble starting the motor and he looked concerned. "I hope the generator isn't acting up," he said aside to me. "I told my uncle to have it checked." Finally, the motor roared to life and we left the dock.

On the way back we made several stops — first at the Ship Museum and then at several historic spots where I took some pictures.

After a spectacular sunset the water turned a cold jade green with whitecaps, and long ribbons of fog hovered over the water like ghostly fingers. I knew fog can come up suddenly on the Cape, blotting out familiar landmarks.

"The boat hasn't much power," Ryan said quietly. "We're going to be late getting in and I had hoped to get the group home before dark." The boat moved slowly but the elderly passengers didn't seem to notice.

Finally, Cora made her way up front. "We're hardly moving. Is something wrong?"

"Everything is all right, Cora. Don't worry," Ryan replied.

Her voice trembled. "You said we would be home by eight. It's already a quarter to nine now."

"We're just running a little late," Ryan said, reassuringly. It grew darker and we were miles from home. I could tell Ryan was worried. The elderly passengers had grown quiet and some complained that they were cold. Ryan told me that blankets were stored overhead and suggested I get them down. I handed them down to Cora and together we tucked them around the passengers who requested them.

Clement beckoned to me. "I don't like the sound of that motor. I think the boy should radio for help."

As he spoke the motor sputtered, stopped, and then started up again. Then it cut out completely and we drifted to a stop. The darkness settled over us like a blanket, and we were without lights or power.

"What happened?" Little cries of alarm sounded from the passengers and I fought down my own panic. The responsibility of twenty senior citizens rested on Ryan and me.

"Please be calm!" Ryan's steady voice was an oasis of confidence in the darkness. "I'm going to call the Coast Guard."

"They could be twenty miles away!" cried a passenger. "They'll never get here in time!"

"I'm radioing my uncle, too, and he'll be starting out to find us," Ryan said calmly. "It's just a matter of time who gets here first. Please don't worry. Help will be on the way."

Someone cried, "The fog's closing in on us! We could be rammed by another boat!" The panic was something you could almost reach out and touch.

I moved among the passengers, putting my arms around them and trying to calm them. "I know you're frightened but try not to alarm the other passengers. Help will be here soon."

"Shannon," Ryan called, "the emergency lanterns are up front. Will you get them out and light them? We're not in danger but as a precaution the passengers should put on their life jackets."

Cries of alarm sounded. "I'll help you with your jackets as soon as the lanterns are lit," I said.

"Maybe we ought to pass the time by singing," a lady suggested timidly.

"I think we ought to pray!" offered another.

"Them that wants to sing can sing and them that wants to pray can pray. As for me, I'm going to light up my last cigar!" Clement struck a match and the light made a small glow in the darkness.

I found the lanterns and switched on the two battery-powered lights while Ryan tried to radio for help. The two gasoline lanterns were harder to light, but with the help of Clement, who made his way painfully up to the front of the boat, we got them going. Shadows from the lanterns flickered over the frightened faces of the passengers.

Cora and I helped the elderly people with their life jackets. A few were able to help themselves but many needed assistance and we buckled the jackets over sweaters and shawls.

A foghorn sounded in the distance and offshore a beam from a lighthouse blinked on and off. The penetrating dampness cut through the thin sweater I wore and I began to shiver. I made my way up to the front of the boat. "Did you reach anyone, Ryan?"

"I contacted both the Coast Guard and my uncle. The Coast Guard is nearly ten miles away. I feel so damned helpless just sitting here and waiting."

"Is there anything more I can do?"

"Just start praying the fog doesn't come up suddenly and swallow us up. They'll never find us if it does."

One of the battery-powered lanterns dimmed and went out; now there were only three lights to pierce the darkness. It was scary drifting in the ink-black water, and the lights on shore seemed far away.

I went back and sat with the passengers. If I could only do something to ease the tension. Then I remembered a time when I was scared half out of my mind. I spoke up. "We've all been in bad situations before but we've survived them. Once I was in an elevator that stalled between floors. It was after five o'clock on a Friday afternoon and I was afraid no one was left in the building. I nearly died of fright and I was sure I would be trapped in the elevator all weekend and that they would find me suffocated Monday morning. A maintenance man making a check a few hours later noticed the elevator was stalled and got me out." I took a deep breath. "We're going to survive this. Tomorrow we'll even joke about it."

"I doubt it," a querulous voice sounded from the back of the boat.

Cora spoke up. "Shannon's right. That's almost as bad as the time I skidded off a country road in a snowstorm and overturned in a ditch. The impact jammed the doors and windows and I couldn't get out. The visibility was almost zero and I knew I was going to freeze to death. About midnight, a fuel oil truck making an emergency delivery to a farmhouse spotted the car and rescued me."

"Things are never as bad as they seem," Clement admitted gruffly.

Other passengers began relating incidents in which they thought their lives had been in danger. It eased some of the tension and the hum of conversation was reassuring as we waited in the darkness. Even Clement told of a storm on the water he had survived as a young man.

About a half-hour later we heard a boat approaching and saw a powerful searchlight cut through the night. "It's my uncle!" Ryan exclaimed, and a cheer went up from the passengers.

The boat drew up alongside of us. "Is everyone all right?" called a heavyset man wearing a captain's cap.

"We're fine!" Clement called out. "We just need a tow!"

"Where's the Coast Guard?" demanded a passenger.

"I just happened to get here first. Now, everyone just stay put and I'll get you home in no time." Ryan's uncle fastened a tow rope to the bow of our boat and we headed for home behind the other boat.

"Row, row, row your boat," someone sang and we all joined in.

"I knew we'd get back safely," I said to Ryan when I joined him up front, "but tonight I'll be as glad as the passengers to get my feet on good solid earth."

"I'm with you," Ryan agreed. "The responsibility of all those people was a pretty big weight on my shoulders."

When we reached the dock, a little crowd had gathered. Someone had intercepted

Ryan's call for help over the marine radio and word had passed around that senior citizens were stranded aboard a tour boat. Many willing hands assisted the elderly people out of the boat onto the dock. Ryan, Cora, and I were the last to leave.

I said, "Cora, for someone who is afraid of water, you came through just fine."

"Honey, I was dying by inches!" she confessed.

With a start I recognized one of the men on the dock as Mr. Harrison. I tried to hurry past him but he stopped me. "Aren't you the young lady who is visiting the Beaumonts this summer?"

"Yes, I am." It was more of a whisper than a normal speaking voice.

Cora spoke up. "I don't know what we would have done without Shannon. She was a great help to us. She just took right over and kept the passengers from panicking."

"You must have fine leadership qualities to take over in an emergency," Mr. Harrison replied. "That calls for strong character."

Oh, wow! I thought. If he only knew.

He continued, "I heard the call come in over my marine radio and I was ready to join the search when I saw the tour boat coming in."

I couldn't think of a single thing to say but he didn't seem to notice. He smiled warmly. "Remember our invitation for brunch. Have Blake bring you over any Sunday. We must get better acquainted."

I found my voice. "Thank you," I stammered and then moved away as gracefully as possible to join Ryan, who was waiting for me. He had heard the conversation and was smiling his Cheshire-cat smile but he didn't make any remarks. I was grateful for that.

Ryan walked me home and we took our time, going over the last hours of the boat trip and recalling how frightening it had been. When we reached the Beaumonts', he said, "I don't want to leave you yet. Isn't there someplace we can talk?"

"There's a gazebo out back in the garden. We could sit there and talk."

"That sounds nice."

We made our way through the garden to the gazebo, an ornate wooden structure partly covered by climbing wisteria vines. The huge purple clusters delicately scented the night air. We sat down on a bench and Ryan reached over and took my hand. "I saw another side of you today, Shannon — a caring, concerned side."

"I'm not all bad, even though I lied to Blake."

"Not bad, just foolish. Sometimes you act as if you haven't another thought in your head except Blake, but watching you care for the elderly people showed me another dimension."

"I've had experience working among elderly people. I'll tell you something if you promise not to laugh."

"Try me," he challenged.

"Back home I belong to a clown band."

A wide grin spread over Ryan's face. "Run that past me again. A clown band?"

"Yes, a clown band. I knew you'd laugh."

"I'm not laughing," he protested.

"Yes, you are," I insisted.

"What instrument do you play?"

"The cymbals. I've had a few lessons on the clarinet but after the girls heard me play they thought I'd better stick to the cymbals."

He was still smiling. "You can't excel at everything. How did this group start?"

"Back in junior high, eight of us girls decided we wanted to do something for other people. We volunteer to entertain at nursing homes, senior citizen centers, and the children's hospital. We're a big hit with the kids."

"You're quite a girl, Shannon."

We sat quietly for a while. I didn't have to be on stage all the time with Ryan. Then he drew me close. "Moonlight becomes you," he whispered huskily.

I smiled. "That sounds old-fashioned but I like it."

He buried his face in the softness of my hair. "You're so beautiful."

"Everyone is beautiful in the moonlight," I answered. The moonlight seemed to be having an effect on me. I was aware of Ryan's closeness, his strong, handsome face. He gave me a long, searching kiss, and for a few seconds I seemed to be all feeling, all sensation. I felt guilty and I drew away. I was Blake's girl and Ryan shouldn't be kissing me like that. I shouldn't be enjoying it, either.

Ryan's voice was unsteady. "I'm sorry. I got carried away. There's a full moon tonight and you know what that does to people."

"I'd better go in now," I said quietly. "Don't complicate things, Ryan. I thought you understood how I feel about Blake right from the beginning."

"You're not mad at me, Shannon?"

"Don't be silly."

Just the same I felt uncomfortable as I let myself into the house with my key and went up to my room. What was the matter with me that I could enjoy the kisses of two boys? I felt I had been unfaithful to Blake.

CHAPTER EIGHT _____

When I came down to breakfast the next morning, Mrs. Beaumont beckoned to me from the study where she was sitting in a flowered housecoat writing letters. "Mr. Beaumont and I have decided to visit my parents in Cambridge this weekend and we plan to take the boys with us. If you wish, you are free to go home for the weekend." She paused. "If you don't want to make the trip home, you are welcome to stay here."

I tried to be cool and keep the excitement out of my voice. "I think I'll stay here. The bus ride home is so boring." What an incredible bit of good luck! I could be with Blake all weekend. I wouldn't have to baby-sit and I could devote all my time to being the girl he thought I was.

"Very well. Rose Marie will be here and you can take your meals with her."

"I'll probably spend all my time on the beach."

She smiled. "It's the Harrison boy, isn't it?"

I felt my color mount and I managed to murmur, "Yes."

"He's a fine young man and so handsome. When we get back from our trip you must ask him over some evening. He might like to watch our home video movies."

I'd have to find a way to prevent *that* from happening.

I expected to see Blake on the beach that afternoon but he didn't show. Had he decided to stay over in Boston another day? I wasn't so naive as to believe that there weren't other girls in his life. They were probably prettier and more sophisticated than I. I felt lonely and a little sad as I watched other couples bobbing in the surf or stretched out on blankets on the sand.

Ryan showed up on the beach, though, with a homemade kite, much to the delight of Robbie and Scott. They raced along the beach with him, their voices blown away by the wind, while the kite plunged and reared like a hooked fish. Finally, it leaped upward and soared, rocking higher and higher while I clapped and cheered.

"Here, you hold the string for a while," Ryan said to Scott. The little boy clutched the string proudly with both hands.

Ryan came over and lay down beside me. I rolled over lazily on the sand and watched the kite, drifting gently as it lifted toward the sun. The gulls wheeled downward, screaming defiantly at it. "I've got about seven rolls of film to be processed, Ryan. You said something about your science teacher offering to let us develop the film in his darkroom."

"Right. Mr. Colburn. When would you like to go over to his house?"

"How about Monday night? If the Beaumonts are at home that evening, I'll be able to get away."

"Monday's fine with me. I'll call him and see if it's okay. I have some rolls of my own to be processed. I'm curious to see how the pictures I took at the wildlife preserve turned out."

I sighed. "My biggest problem is to think as a photographer, not as a tourist. I get carried away by anything of historic interest. I hope the pictures won't look too amateurish."

"Mr. Colburn can give us some tips. He freelances for the local newspapers."

I heard a horn beep and looked up to see Blake in his silver gray sports car. "Hi!" he called.

"Watch the boys for me a minute, Ryan!" I jumped up and ran across the sand to the road. I gave Blake a quick kiss.

"I just got back, love. Jerome and I met some friends in Boston and we decided to stay over for a day."

"I'm glad you're back. I missed you." It was all I could do to keep from touching him.

"I see Ryan is still hanging around," Blake said, looking over at the beach. "Have you been seeing him while I was away?"

"I spent yesterday on the tour boat with him. You'll hear about it from your dad. We had to be towed back."

"That figures. Where does my dad fit in?" Blake asked.

"He was on the dock to help us. We had a boatload of senior citizens."

Blake looked over at the beach where Ryan was helping Scott reel in the kite. "Ryan doesn't lose any time moving in while I'm out of town."

"I didn't ask what you did while you were away, Blake."

"I'll tell you. Yesterday we spent most of the day on campus, took in a show at night, and ate a lot of ethnic food; and today I bought some records and some clothes for school. Do you believe me?"

"Of course," I answered.

"Hop in the car and ride home with me. We can listen to records and I'll show you the new blazer I bought."

"I can't. I'm watching the boys." I saw the disappointment in his face and added quickly, "But I didn't make any plans for Saturday and Sunday. I'm saving both days for you."

"Suppose you get stuck taking care of the boys?"

"Not a chance. The Beaumonts are going away for the weekend and taking the children along."

"She's going to miss you when you leave. She'll have to hire a baby-sitter," Blake replied. "I'll pick you up tomorrow morning and we'll spend the whole day together."

"I'll be ready."

"And Shannon, tell Ryan to go fly a kite someplace else."

"I think you're jealous."

"You got it!" he smiled. He gunned the motor and took off, wheels spinning and sending up a shower of gravel from the shoulder of the road.

The Beaumonts left for Cambridge about five o'clock, Robbie clutching Poo Dog and crying because I wasn't going along. As I watched them leave, I felt like spinning around the room like a whirling dervish. I was elated at the thought that I could do anything I wanted to for the next two days.

Rose Marie and I ate supper together and later in the evening, after I washed my hair and did my nails, I watched TV with her. Rose Marie liked the game shows while I preferred a good movie; we ended up watching the contestants bouncing around on the stage like rubber balls and showing off their greed.

During a commercial, Rose Marie said, "You only have a few more weeks on the Cape. What's going to happen to you and the Harrison boy?"

"We talked it over and I think we'll keep seeing each other," I answered.

"College will be a whole new life for him. Boys change. I saw it happen with my sister's boys."

Why did she have to stir up my insecure

feelings when I was looking forward to a great weekend with Blake? Suddenly I blurted out, "Blake thinks I'm a guest here. He doesn't know I'm the baby-sitter."

She looked at me sternly. "And how did you manage that, young lady?"

"With a few lies." My voice broke on that word — *lies*. "I was just trying to impress Blake. I've never known anyone like him before."

"That explains a few things that have happened lately. How do you think this intrigue is going to end?"

I started to cry. "I don't know, but please don't tell him or the Beaumonts! Please!"

Her voice was reproachful. "I won't lie for you. I've worked here six summers for the Beaumonts and I owe them my loyalty."

"I'm not asking you to lie for me. Just don't mention to Blake that I'm the baby-sitter."

She looked grim. "You certainly have a talent for getting yourself into trouble, Shannon McCabe."

"I'm not really like this. I just messed things up the first day I met Blake and now I'm stuck with it."

"You could tell him the truth. You can't drag this charade on forever," she said severely.

"He might not want to see me anymore!"

"You know he'll find out sooner or later." One of the game show contestants had just won a vacation to Curaçao, but Rose Marie had lost interest in the show.

"Don't you see — I love him!"

"I don't approve of this one bit."

"Just for the weekend, please!" I begged. Couldn't she understand? Hadn't she ever loved someone so much that nothing else mattered?

She didn't answer right away and the moments dragged by, trailing suspense behind them. Then she said, "I'll have to think about it. You're one foolish girl."

I went over and put my arm around her. "Please don't let me down. Maybe I'll tell Blake this weekend."

I said good night to her and went up to my room. Now four people knew I was a phony — Ryan, Mac, Jamie, and Rose Marie.

Saturday was a lovely day, not too hot. Blake came to the house for me around ten o'clock, wearing cut-off jeans and a faded blue sweat shirt. He stood, hands tucked into the slanted pockets of the shirt. "Are you in the mood for a picnic?"

"I'll picnic anywhere with you," I answered cheerfully.

"That's my girl. I had the cook pack us a picnic lunch. We'll find some secluded spot where we can swim, loaf around, and listen to music."

"Sounds great. I'll get my bikini. Shall I bring something along for the picnic? Potato chips? Pretzels?"

"No. My parents had a party last night and there were plenty of terrific leftovers. We don't need a thing."

I ran upstairs and put my bikini in my

beach bag along with my sunglasses and camera. I wanted to take pictures of Blake today. Lots of them.

When I came downstairs Rose Marie came to the door and gave a little curtsy. "Is there anything you would like me to do for you today, Miss Shannon?"

I felt my cheeks grow warm. Rose Marie was giving me the needle. "No, thank you, Rose Marie."

I caught a glimpse of mischief in her eyes. "Are there any special dishes you would like me to prepare for dinner?"

Blake spoke up. "Don't plan on Shannon for dinner. We may be late getting home."

"Very well, sir." Rose Marie gave another little curtsy and went into the kitchen.

We walked down the road to Blake's house and I waited while he went inside and came out with a picnic hamper that he put into a Chris Craft tied up at the dock. He helped me into the boat and revved up the motor. The sleek little craft glided away from the pier.

We passed an abandoned lighthouse with its foundations wreathed in seaweed, and headed out into the open water. I watched the familiar landmarks of Piedmont Point grow smaller and smaller until they were hardly more than a smudge in the distance. I was content just to lie back among the cushions and watch Blake. I liked his expert handling of the boat, the dark bronze of his skin, the smile he flashed back at me.

When my forehead began to burn from

the sun I looked around and found a cap
with a visor. "You look like an outfielder,"
Blake laughed.

"Where are we going?" I asked. I was getting hungry and I was curious about the con-
tents of the picnic hamper. What did rich
people take along on picnics?

"A special place I have in mind."

"Another special place?" I asked. "How
many do you have?"

"Look ahead." A little island lay ahead of
us, rising out of the water as if it were waiting for us. When we came near, Blake cut
the motor and we drifted toward it. "How
about it?" he smiled. "Our private island."

The trees on the island were fringed by a
white sandy beach and I could hear the cat-
like cries of the herring gulls. "Have you ever
been here before?" I asked.

"Many times," he smiled.

"With a girl?"

He reached over and mussed my hair.
"Now who's jealous?"

Blake dropped anchor and we waded
ashore carrying the picnic hamper, my beach
bag, a blanket, and the cassette player.
"Here's a good spot," Blake said, setting
down the hamper and spreading out the
blanket. It was peaceful and quiet, and the
sun shining through the trees made patterns
on the blanket.

"Let's take a swim before we eat." Blake
had discarded his sweat shirt in the boat and
now he took off his cut-off jeans. He was
wearing bathing trunks underneath.

I took my camera out of my beach bag. "Let me take your picture, Blake."

He struck a Mr. Universe stance — arms raised, fists clenched. "How's this?"

"I want something serious," I scolded.

He sat down on a log and assumed the pose of Rodin's sculpture *The Thinker*, bending slightly forward with his head on his hand.

"Come on, Blake. Something romantic."

"Something you can blow up into a poster and hang on the wall of your dorm room at Sunderlin's?"

Why did he have to remind me of my lies? I bent my head, pretending to be busy adjusting the camera lens. Blake wouldn't take me seriously but kept playing around. "I want a picture of you and me together," he said.

"Sorry. I don't have my tripod here. Please — just one natural pose of you. Maybe over by the boat."

"I'm no male model. Let's go swimming."

"After I get my pictures."

Blake was serious for a full two minutes and I got some great shots of him — pictures that would make my friends at home tear out their hair with envy. "Okay," I said when I had finished the roll. "Where will I change?"

"There's a clump of trees over there."

I hesitated. "I won't look," he assured me, laughing.

"Suppose someone is camping on the island?"

"The only campers around here are the hermit crabs."

I went into the thicket and watched over my shoulder as I changed. Blake was already in the water and I swam out to meet him. The water was cool and invigorating, and we swam in unison, stroke for stroke. But Blake had to goof off. He would disappear under the water for so long I was sure he had drowned and I would start to panic. Then he'd suddenly bob up in front of me, shaking the water from his head, laughing.

"Have you ever been kissed underwater?" he asked. He pulled me beneath the water and kissed me. It was a strange sensation, a sort of underwater fantasy. Everything was green and shimmery like a Jacques Cousteau film. I knew my long, dark hair was floating straight up.

"You looked like a mermaid underwater," Blake said when we surfaced. "Let's hit the beach. I'm hungry."

After we toweled each other off we sat down on the blanket and Blake opened the hamper. He took out some tiny sandwiches with the crusts cut off, cheese, little vegetables like cherry tomatoes and celery curls to munch on, a clam dip, and some bite-sized party cakes.

"Here's the wine!" He held up a bottle of white wine. Moisture was dripping down the side of the bottle and I could see it had been chilled.

"Wine? For a picnic?"

Blake leaned over and gave me a quick kiss on the cheek. "You didn't think I'd bring beer for an elegant picnic with you, did you?"

We munched on the little sandwiches and dipped the celery curls in the clam dip. Everything tasted so good. The cook had even packed fresh strawberries and peeled slices of ripe cantaloupe.

Blake opened the wine and poured some into a cup. "It's a fairly sweet wine. Almost like punch."

"I'll bet!" I laughed but took the cup. I didn't want him to think I wasn't sophisticated. My parents didn't drink and never served any alcoholic beverages except to guests on very special occasions.

The coolness felt good on my throat. Blake raised his glass. "To Shannon — who changed my summer." I felt that rush of tenderness again. This was a romantic picnic. I thought of other picnics I had been on with the burned hot dogs, the soggy salads, the lukewarm lemonade, the ants. But this — this was living!

"Do you like the wine?" Blake asked, filling up my cup again.

"It's very nice." I was beginning to feel warm and mellow.

"Love me?" he asked, moving closer. He took my cup and set it in the sand. Then he kissed me, a slow, deliberate kiss, and it was the most exciting kiss we had ever shared. I pressed my lips back warmly and we kissed a long time. I felt hypnotized by his closeness and my kisses were just as meaningful as his. I couldn't get enough of them.

Then Blake's embrace became more intense and I pushed him away. Hard.

He rolled over on his back. "I'm not a Ken doll, Shannon. I have feelings. Don't you know I care for you deeply?"

"I'm sorry." I felt inadequate and a disappointment to him.

"Don't you care for me at all?"

I sat very still, hardly breathing. I wanted to chose my words very carefully. "I like you, Blake, but you'll be going away to college and I may never see you again."

"You know that's not true. Of course I'll be seeing you. Have you ever watched the stars all night with a boy or watched the sun come up?"

It was such a temptation it hurt. I couldn't bear to look at him.

He continued, "We could spend the night on the beach. I have blankets in the boat. Nothing has to happen. I just want to be with you."

I probably sounded like something out of a Victorian novel but it was the way I felt. "Love doesn't have to be rushed. I want ours to develop slowly. I don't want to spend the night on the beach with you. You do understand, don't you?"

"You talk as if what we feel for each other is just infatuation."

"I think it's more than that. I just want to be sure."

"You're too much!" There was a sharp edge to Blake's voice. I felt awkward and ill at ease. Had I handled it badly?

He poured himself a full cup of wine and downed it. Then he stood up and started walking along the beach, stopping occasionally to send a stone skimming over the water.

I sat hugging my knees, feeling miserable. Why couldn't boys be satisfied with just kisses? What did you do when you wanted to please a boy and yet hang on to your own beliefs? Was Blake used to girls who were more accommodating?

After a long time he came back and went into the water, swimming so far out that I became frightened. It was too soon after he had eaten and he had drunk all that wine. Suppose he had a cramp when he was out so far. I couldn't ever reach him in time. I didn't even know how to start the boat.

He didn't look at me when he came back, but lay down on the sand with his back to me. I gathered up the remains of our picnic lunch and put it in the hamper. I fed the crumbs to the gulls. When Blake's even breathing told me he was asleep, I turned on the cassette player softly and lay down beside him. After a while I slept.

When I awoke the sun was low in the sky and Blake was putting our things in the boat. When he saw I was awake he came over and took both of my hands. "It's okay. Let's forget what I said earlier. You have a right to your own standards."

I felt better now that he had spoken. I

couldn't bear to end this beautiful day on a bad note.

He said, "We're not going to let it spoil our day."

"We have so few left," I agreed.

"I know, less than two weeks. We don't want to waste any of them." He helped me to my feet. "We'd better get going. We have a long ride home."

We were both quiet on the ride home. At Rock Harbor we stopped at a little restaurant for pizza and while we were waiting Blake put some money in the jukebox and we danced. It was country music, pulsing with emotion, and it was the first time I had ever danced with Blake. He put both arms around me, holding me close, and I just gave myself over to the music as our bodies moved as one. I watched the silver levers of the record changer swing and dip behind the glass like the arms of a robot.

It was nearly eleven o'clock when he brought me home. "Will you come in?" I asked. I didn't think Rose Marie would care if I asked him.

"I don't think so. Thanks just the same."

Would he ask me out again or had he decided there wasn't anyplace for me in his life? I had to find out. "Will I see you tomorrow?"

"I promised you the weekend. How about that trip to Provincetown?"

"What time should I be ready?"

"Around nine o'clock. We should get an early start."

104

Rose Marie was waiting up for me, reading a paperback romance. "Well?" she asked expectantly.

"I had a perfectly wonderful day," I replied, starting up the stairs. I didn't feel like talking.

"Did you tell Blake?"

"No, not yet."

"Hummmmmm." She settled back in her chair. "I don't need a crystal ball to see there's trouble ahead for you, girl."

I put both hands over my ears and ran upstairs.

CHAPTER NINE _____

Sunday morning we drove up the coast to Provincetown. As we neared the town, traffic was bumper to bumper. "I like to come up here in the late autumn or winter when the tourists are gone," Blake remarked. "Commercialism is ruining places like Hyannis, Buzzards Bay, and Provincetown. It's turning them into glorified travel brochures and traffic jams."

We parked and took a walking tour of the town, up the narrow streets lined with gift shops, sidewalk art shows, antique stores, and tawdry little shops selling junk art. There were all kinds of people — freaky weirdos with punk haircuts and miniskirts mixed with square tourists in Bermuda shorts and knee socks.

The town wasn't what I expected. I had pictured sea captains with rolling gaits and Portuguese fishermen just in from a cod run, clumping over the boardwalks in rubber boots.

"This used to be an artist colony — at least that's what they tell me," Blake said, "but now it's been taken over by pseudo artists and artsy-craftsy types. Will you look at some of that junk?" He pointed to crocheted dolls in garish colors designed to cover rolls of toilet tissue.

"What happened to the real artists and writers?"

"They probably packed up their palettes and typewriters and moved on." We wandered through stores with names like Ye Olde Wood Shoppe and Mother Earth Crafts. I bought a few souvenirs — a belt buckle with a western motif for Ben, some postcards, and a beach ball for Scott and Robbie. In a handcraft shop, I found an over-the-shoulder purse in beige with a polished wooden handle for Rose Marie. I hoped she would like it.

In the afternoon we sat on the grass and ate popcorn at an open-air theater where students were putting on a Gilbert and Sullivan musical. They were good and so dedicated. I hoped that somehow they would all realize their dreams.

From a sidewalk craftsman Blake picked out an opal pendant on a silver chain. He held it up. "Do you like it, Shannon?"

"It's beautiful!" The sun caught the fiery colors of the stone.

"We'll take it," he said to the bearded

young man. Blake fastened it around my neck. "To remember our summer."

No one had ever bought me jewelry before. Not even my parents or grandparents. They had bought me presents like tennis rackets or radios or hair dryers, but never jewelry. I had bought my school ring for myself.

It wasn't until later that I remembered my grandmother said opals were bad luck. They represented tears. I hoped it was just an old wives' tale.

Later, over tacos at an outdoor café, Blake said, "I'm thinking of asking Ryan to sail with me in the boat race Labor Day weekend. Do you think he will?"

"What day is the race?"

"The Sunday before the holiday."

"You'll have to ask Ryan. He may have to work," I replied.

"My brother and I have always sailed together, but this year he's leaving for college early."

"Where does he go?" I asked.

"Berkeley. He's a senior there. I'm going to miss his help. We won last year and we had some stiff competition."

"The race must be important to you."

"It is. I'm competitive by nature. I like to win," he smiled.

"If Ryan doesn't have to work he'll probably sail with you," I said.

"Ryan and I used to sail together as kids and he really knows how to handle a boat." Blake ordered a second taco. "By the way,

Jerome and Gina want to double-date with us some night. How about it?"

This was another obstacle but I was sure I could handle it. My luck was holding out and I was becoming confident. "Sounds great. I'm busy tomorrow night. Ryan and I are developing some film. His science teacher is letting us use his darkroom and equipment."

"Ryan and you in a darkroom? Now, there's a heavy situation."

"It's all very professional. After all, photography will be my career."

Blake frowned. "Ryan seems to be turning up quite often."

"Some people have trouble believing a boy and girl can just be friends," I said. Why couldn't Blake understand?

"I suppose I have to overlook it if I want Ryan to sail with me, but I can't help resenting it when he's with you."

I changed the subject. "How about Thursday for our date with Jerome and Gina?" Thursday was my day off and it would simplify matters.

"You've got it. I thought we could have dinner and go someplace later. There's a really good band that night at Gandy's."

We drove home along the National Seashore and it was a beautiful ride. We stopped at an outdoor restoration of a seventeenth-century Pilgrim village and walked along a dusty street lined with wooden houses surrounded by fenced gardens. We smelled wood smoke, saw food cooking, and watched people carrying on the daily tasks of an early farming community. It was like seeing a chapter from a history book come to life.

When we reached home and pulled into the driveway Blake said, "I wonder whose car that is."

I had been riding with my head on his shoulder and when I looked up my heart nearly stopped beating. The old green Pinto with the rusted fenders was my parents' car! What were they doing here? If Blake connected that old wreck of a car with my parents it was all over. The owners of that car could never be friends of the Beaumonts or send a daughter to Sunderlin's.

"It's only nine o'clock. Are you going to ask me in?" Blake remarked. "We could watch TV. There's a good movie on cable tonight that I've been wanting to see."

I was nearly immobilized with panic. I managed to find my voice. "Not tonight."

"Why? Does that car belong to a boyfriend from back home?"

"Don't be silly. I told you there was no one else." I reached for the door handle again but he caught my arm. "What's wrong? You're acting weird again. Sometimes you act as if you're two different girls."

"I really must go." Suppose my brother Ben saw me in the car and came running out!

"What's the hurry? Can't we sit and talk?"

"I'm tired. I'll call you in the morning, Blake."

"Didn't you have a good time today?" He sounded hurt.

"I loved every minute of it."

"Then what's wrong?" He kissed me but I couldn't respond. My anxiety left me as lifeless as a figure in a wax museum. Why had my parents come here? Why did they have to spoil everything?

I edged toward the door. "Thanks for everything today." I opened the car door and ran up the walk to the house, hearing Blake squeal his tires as the car took off. I had to ring the bell, for Rose Marie kept the house tightly secured.

She came to the door. "It's about time! Your folks have been here since five o'clock, waiting for you."

The moment I saw my parents and Ben I was overcome with remorse. How could I have resented them for coming here? What a crummy person I was becoming!

I went over and kissed them. "We wanted to surprise you," Mom said. "We didn't stop to think you might have other plans."

"I couldn't wait to tell you I got a job in New London," Dad added. He looked so happy. I gave him a big hug. I was so pleased he had found work, even if it meant we would have to move.

Mom continued, "We thought we'd take a little vacation before Dad starts his job." She was wearing her old pink pants suit with a big, jeweled pin on the lapel.

"I begin working the Tuesday after Labor

Day," my dad said. "We're staying at the Sandy Beach Motel just outside of town. We thought it would be nice to see you and meet the Beaumonts and then move on up the coast to visit your Aunt Margaret in Eastham."

"Where're those boyfriends of yours with the boats? I want to meet them," Ben said.

"Ryan may be working tomorrow," I answered.

"Is he the one with the speedboat?" Ben asked.

"No, that's Blake."

"He's the one I really want to meet."

"We'll see," I hedged.

"We brought our fishing rods. I hear the fishing's great here," my dad remarked.

Rose Marie went out to the kitchen to make coffee and my dad came over and sat beside me on the love seat. "You seem a little worried, Shannon. Is something wrong?"

"No, no. I guess I'm not over my surprise at seeing you. When are we moving?"

"Your mother and I talked it over and we decided to let you finish your senior year at Madison High. I'll get a small apartment in New London and come home weekends."

My parents loved me and would make this sacrifice for me. It made me feel worse than ever. "It's not fair to you, Dad."

"It's only for a year. You're doing so well at Madison, and we don't want to jeopardize your chances of getting into a good college."

"That makes me feel guilty," I protested. "You'll be lonesome alone in New London,

Dad. You know Ben needs you, too. Don't do it just for my sake."

"The year will go by before we know it, and in the meantime I'll be looking for a new home for us in New London."

"I have some news, too," my mother said. "I'm going to enroll in some refresher courses at the university this fall; I plan on going back to teaching when we move."

I looked at Dad. What did he think?

He smiled and said, "Your mother wants to do her thing and we're all going to help her."

Some good *had* come from this critical period my parents had gone through. Dad realized my mother had goals she had a right to pursue. "I can take over some of the housework while you're studying, Mom," I said.

"We'll work something out," she smiled. "You'll be busy this year, too."

Rose Marie came in with coffee and blueberry kuchen. After we had visited awhile, and Rose Marie and my mother had exchanged favorite recipes, my parents left, promising to see me tomorrow.

Up in my room I undressed for bed. I couldn't bear to take off the opal necklace. Maybe my grandmother was right. Opals *were* bad luck. I had decided one thing tonight as I sat downstairs with my parents. I wasn't going to sell them short. If Blake found out the truth about me through their visit, that is the way it would have to be. The sacrifice they were making for me had struck home tonight and I would not lie about them.

If Blake happened to meet them, he would see them for what they were — hardworking, middle-class parents. And I would not go out of my way to avoid Blake's meeting them. I loved my parents.

Blake called early the next morning. "Are you in a better mood this morning, Shannon?"

"I'm sorry. I was abrupt last night," I apologized.

"That's an understatement. How would you like to play tennis this morning?"

"My parents are here and I'm spending the day with them."

"Are they staying with the Beaumonts?" he asked.

"No, they're staying at a motel," I replied.

"A motel! Why can't the Beaumonts put them up?"

"They're not home." I felt uneasy.

"It seems as if they could have made some arrangements. How long have your parents known the Beaumonts?"

"Not too long." This wasn't really a lie but I wasn't being exactly honest, either.

"Look, we have two guest cottages and neither one is in use this week," Blake said.

"No! I'm sure my parents are perfectly content where they are!"

"But it's foolish for them to stay at a motel. Wait, I'll ask my mother." He was insistent.

"Blake! No — my parents are leaving in the morning. Thanks just the same."

"Okay, if that's the way you feel about it,

but they are perfectly welcome to use the cottage," he said. I could just see my folks driving up to the Harrisons' cottage in their rusted-out Pinto and carrying their battered suitcases up the driveway. I wasn't ashamed of my parents. I just didn't want anyone snubbing them.

"Give me a rain check on that tennis date," I said.

"If you went to a tennis camp last year, you must be pretty good."

"I'll give you a good game," I answered.

"We'll get together later in the week. Don't forget our date with Jerome and Gina on Thursday."

"Sure thing." I felt a calmness, as if whatever happened today was inevitable.

I went downstairs and gave Rose Marie the purse I had bought for her in Provincetown. "Is this for keeping my mouth shut over the weekend?" She examined it carefully and I could tell she was pleased.

"Of course not. I told you I was going to buy you a present."

"It's handmade. I can tell. Beige is a good color. White gets too dirty and it looks out of place after Labor Day." She gave me a hug. "Thanks, honey."

The Beaumonts arrived home about ten o'clock and I helped carry their luggage into the house. Robbie and Scott were glad to see me and wanted to go to the beach. Mrs. Beaumont called me aside. "Rose Marie tells me your parents are in town. After you unpack the boys' things and put them away, you can have the rest of the day off to spend with your family."

I thanked her and decided she might not be too bad after all. Rich people were just different.

"Do you have any plans for the day?" she asked.

"I thought they might like a ride on the tour boat," I answered.

"A splendid idea. I can also recommend some excellent restaurants in the area."

I introduced her to my parents when they arrived and she was very pleasant. "My, what a gracious lady," my mother said, when we left the house and headed toward the dock. "And such a lovely home. I'm sure this has been an enriching experience for you, Shannon."

Oh, sure, I thought. What would my mother think if she knew what a phony her only daughter was?

The tour boat was filling up for the eleven o'clock boat trip advertised in the brochure as a "three-hour Cape Cod adventure." I silently agreed that the senior citizen trip had been an adventure! Ryan insisted we go along as guests and he wouldn't accept the money my father offered him for the tickets.

Ben wasn't too thrilled about taking the tour. "I want to meet the guy with the speedboat," he complained. "This clunker probably doesn't go over fifteen miles an hour."

I gave him a poke. "Be quiet. It's free. Later you can meet Blake if he's home."

My folks enjoyed the tour. It was all new to them and Ryan made several unscheduled stops so they could go ashore and visit some historic spots.

When we got back, Ben was still making a pest of himself about the speedboat. My dad spoke up. "Why don't you take him to meet your friend? Your mother and I will visit the boat museum Ryan told us about and we'll meet back here at five for dinner."

Ryan came over before we left. "Shall I call Mr. Colburn and ask him if we can use the darkroom another night? He was expecting us tonight."

"I forgot all about it, Ryan. Will tomorrow night do just as well? I'll check with Mrs. Beaumont."

"No sweat. I'll call you tomorrow. Enjoy your dinner."

"Thanks for the tour, Ryan. My parents really enjoyed it."

Ben looked the way most fourteen-year-old boys look whether they're from a farm, New York City, or Piedmont Point — scuffed sneakers, jeans, and a faded sweat shirt. If Blake asked Ben any questions, would he blow my cover? The calmness I had felt earlier in the day had left me, and my stomach felt like raw hamburger.

When we reached the Harrisons', the housekeeper answered our knock. "I believe you'll find Blake down at the dock."

"Thanks. We'll look for him," I replied.

Ben exclaimed as we walked over the lush, green lawn. "You didn't tell me Blake was rich. They even have their own tennis court. Wow!"

We found Blake working on one of the boats. "Blake, this is my brother Ben."

Blake held out a greasy hand. "Hello, Ben."

"He's made a nuisance of himself ever since I told him about your speedboat."

Ben was examining the boat. "How fast does it go?"

"Shall we take it out and open it up?"

"All right!"

"May I wait on shore?" I asked. "I'm no speed freak."

"Chicken!" Blake laughed.

"Put on a life jacket, Ben," I insisted.

"Oh, for Pete's sake!"

"Just like a sister," Blake said, "but let's humor her. Put on a jacket, Ben."

I sat on the pier and watched the boat skimming over the water. Would the confrontation come with Blake today? Had I finally reached the end of my rope? Maybe it would work out all right and Blake wouldn't ask Ben too many questions.

I scanned Blake's face when they pulled up at the dock a half-hour later but he was laughing. I hoped that meant my secret was still safe.

"Thanks for taking Ben out on the water, Blake."

"What's your hurry?"

"We're meeting my parents for dinner at five," I replied.

"If Ben was going to be around a few more days I'd teach him to water-ski."

"Maybe some other time. We really have to go now," I said.

"You're the boss," Blake replied.

As Ben and I walked home I asked, "Did Blake say anything about me?"

"He wanted to know if you had a boyfriend back home."

"What did you say?"

"I said there was one guy but he wasn't anything special," Ben answered.

"Thanks a lot! What else did he say?"

Ben shrugged. "We didn't talk much. The boat makes so much noise you have to yell."

We had dinner in a restaurant called the Blue Dolphin and it was good to see my parents so relaxed and happy. They had so many plans for the future.

My dad said, "I think we'll start out for your Aunt Margaret's tonight. We have a few hours of daylight left and we should make it there by nine-thirty."

"Do you have next weekend off, Shannon?" my mother asked.

"I may have to work since Mrs. Beaumont gave me this weekend off," I replied.

"Well, you'll be coming home for good in a few days and we can't wait to have you back."

When my parents left, I felt quite pleased with myself. Luck had been with me all day. I hadn't tried to hide my parents. Circumstances had just worked in my favor.

CHAPTER TEN

Ryan called when I was back at the Beaumonts'. "Have your parents left?"

"Yes. They decided to start out tonight."

"Still want to develop the film tonight?"

"I'd forgotten all about it. Wait, I'll check with Mrs. Beaumont."

I asked if I could have the evening off. She said that they would be home and it would be all right for me to go out. "Is it the Harrison boy?" she asked coyly.

"No. Ryan Webster and I are developing film at his science teacher's home."

"I didn't know you were interested in photography," she replied.

"I've taken seven rolls of film this summer and quite a few pictures are of Scott and Robbie. Children are wonderful subjects."

"I hope you'll show them to me."

I felt flattered. "I'll make you some prints if the pictures turn out well."

"I'd like that." She paused. "Don't be shy about inviting Blake over to watch our video movies."

I went back to the phone. "I can have the evening off, Ryan."

"Good. I'll borrow my father's car. The Colburns live about three miles outside town."

Ryan and I bought the supplies we needed for developing and printing the pictures, and drove over to Mr. Colburn's home. Mr. Colburn lived in a new housing development. We parked in the driveway and sidestepped tricycles, a doll with one arm, some trailer trucks, and a plastic cycle.

"He has four kids," Ryan explained.

"No way!" I said.

"Don't be sarcastic." Ryan rang the doorbell and a bearded young man in paint-spattered jeans came to the door, holding a paintbrush.

"I hope we didn't come at the wrong time," Ryan said.

"It's quite all right. If you two know what you're doing, I'll leave you alone and go back to painting the bathroom." He led us downstairs to the darkroom — a small space off the basement family room. "I think you'll find everything you need, but if you don't, call me. I'll look in on you later."

We unpacked our supplies and set up the equipment. "I hope you've done this before," Ryan remarked, as he prepared the developing tank under my instructions.

"Trust me."

"I've never developed film before. I've always taken my film to the drugstore," he said.

"Then you're going to learn something today." I showed him how to run the film through the developing tank. Then we hung the film up with clips to dry, wiping off the excess water with a sponge. The work was painstaking and we worked quickly, hardly talking.

When the negatives were dry I exposed them to light to develop. After developing we washed them in an acid bath, followed by a water bath. Finally, we laid the pictures upside down on a clean blotter.

We had made over one hundred forty prints and I stepped back to admire our work. "Not bad for a couple of amateurs. Do you know what it would have cost us at the drugstore?"

"Plenty," Ryan agreed.

"About sixty dollars. All it cost us was the supplies. And now that you understand the technique, you can do your own developing and printing."

My summer memories lay before me — beach pictures, pictures taken of Blake on our island picnic, the senior citizen tour, pictures of Scott and Robbie. Ryan's wildlife prints turned out beautifully, and I was sure I could learn a lot from him about exposure and using filters.

I picked up a picture of Clement. "I promised to make some extra prints of the tour for the senior citizens."

"By the way," said Ryan, "I saw Cora yesterday and she said they're having a birthday party for Clement on Wednesday and we're invited. It's at the Center," he explained.

"Oh, can we go, Ryan? It would be a good time to take the pictures over. I'd like to take Clement a present, too. He did try to help us on the boat."

He smiled a Cheshire-cat grin. "We can go. It's too bad you don't have your clown suit."

"You still think that's funny," I said indignantly.

"I'm just teasing you. We'd better come back another evening to make the extra prints. It's ten-thirty and Mr. Colburn might want to go to bed. He works at the post office during summer vacation."

As we were cleaning the equipment, Mr. Colburn came in. "How are you kids doing?"

"Cleaning up. Take a look at the prints and tell us what you think," Ryan said.

Mr. Colburn bent over the prints. "On the whole they are quite good. The pictures of the sunset are a bit overexposed, and if you had used a reflector on the barn pictures it would have softened the harsh contrasts." Then he picked up the picture of Scott and Robbie examining a sand dollar. "This is an excellent study. Who took it?"

"I did," I answered.

He held the picture up. "The best pictures of children are taken when they are not aware of what you're doing. Look at how natural the children are — there's no hint of

123

posing. The lighting and background are perfect." He turned to me. "The local newspaper I freelance for is sponsoring an amateur photo contest. If you don't mind, I'd like to enter the picture in the contest for you."

"I'd be honored," I said, with a hint of pride in my voice. I was really pleased with myself, even though the picture had been a stroke of good luck.

He found a pad and pencil. "I'll need the boys' names."

"Scott and Robbie Beaumont, 144 Beach Avenue."

"Your name?"

"Shannon McCabe, same address."

"I saw several other pictures I'd like to enter." Mr. Colburn picked out a wildlife photo of a heron with an interesting pattern of seashore plants in the background. The other picture was a harbor scene taken at sunrise. Both prints were Ryan's.

"Is it all right if we come back another night and make some extra prints?" Ryan asked.

"Of course. Leave the photos here to dry thoroughly. No one will disturb them," Mr. Colburn said.

"Maybe tomorrow night. How about it, Shannon?" Ryan asked.

"Okay by me."

Outside, I gave Ryan a hug. "Mr. Colburn thought our pictures were good enough for the contest! I forgot to ask him what the prizes were."

"Don't lose any sleep over it. We'll have

some stiff competition from the summer people with their expensive cameras."

"I don't think they'll bother to enter a local contest. No class."

"I noticed you took a lot of pictures of Blake. What are you going to do? Blow them up poster size?"

"That's an idea," I agreed.

"You didn't take a picture of me."

"Well take care of that tomorrow on the beach. Maybe I'll blow you up to poster size, too. You're an important part of my summer," I assured him.

"Do you mean that?" he asked.

"You know I do. By the way, I understand Blake is going to ask you to sail with him in the race on Labor Day weekend."

"That's the first I've heard about it. His brother always sails with him. They're a winning team."

"He's leaving for college early this year. Can you help Blake out?" I asked. I wasn't sure how Ryan felt about Blake.

"There's a lot of prestige connected with winning that race. I wouldn't mind being a part of it," he admitted.

"Isn't the holiday weekend busy for you on the tour boat?" I asked.

"We schedule extra trips, but if I let my uncle know in time he could hire someone to help out. He wouldn't be happy about it but I haven't taken time off this summer."

We rode home slowly through the darkened streets and Ryan took the long way home, past the golf course and the boat yards. I pretended not to notice. Maybe he wanted to talk.

Finally he spoke. "You'll soon be gone with the rest of the summer people, maybe out of my life forever."

"We can keep in touch, Ryan," I reassured him.

"You won't be back next year, will you?"

"No, I won't come back to Piedmont Point. At least not to baby-sit," I answered.

"Perhaps to see Blake?"

"Ryan, by next summer you will have found someone else."

He wouldn't look at me. "If the world ended tomorrow, I'd still love you."

I said firmly, "A year from now you may wonder why you ever said that. You'll be leaving for college and have a whole new world ahead of you. A good-looking guy like you won't have to worry about finding girls."

"You don't understand," he said quietly. "You don't understand at all."

I didn't like to hurt people but I had to tell him how I felt. It would have been wrong to lead Ryan on.

The next two days passed quietly. Blake drove his father to Maine on a business trip and was gone for two days. As a result I saw more of Ryan. We went to Mr. Colburn's Tuesday night and made more prints of the pictures he wanted, and Wednesday we drove over to the Center for Clement's birthday party. The senior citizens who had been on the tour boat greeted us with enthusiasm and gathered around the pictures.

We ate homemade birthday cake, drank punch, and listened to the retelling of the boat trip and how well we had handled it. Ryan and I had picked out presents for Clement—a twin pack of playing cards for his euchre games and a box of candy.

He seemed to be embarrassed. "You didn't have to buy an old fellow like me anything." I knew he was pleased. I saw tears glistening in his bright blue eyes.

As we drove home I said to Ryan, "I enjoy working with older people. Perhaps my life would be more meaningful if I planned a career in geriatrics instead of photography."

"What's geriatrics?" he asked.

"Well, to quote the dictionary, it's an area of medical practice concerned with the physiological and health problems of the elderly."

"That's heavy but I think you could do it. You care about people." He paused. "On the other hand, I would hate to see you give up your photography."

"I could never give up photography completely, even though I know the field is overcrowded. Well, I have a year to make up my mind."

I decided I'd give Mrs. Beaumont prints of the better pictures I had taken of Scott and Robbie when I left on Labor Day, as sort of a going-away present. I had no hint of the trouble one of those pictures was going to bring me.

CHAPTER ELEVEN _____

On Thursday I took a long time getting ready for our double date with Jerome and Gina, because I wanted Blake to be proud of me when he introduced me to his friends. I showered, blow-dried my hair, and did the world's fastest job of shortening one of the pairs of designer jeans Mrs. Beaumont had given me. It was cool enough that I could wear the soft, pale gray sweater I had bought at the boutique when I was paid last week. The opal pendant looked lovely against the sweater. I brushed my hair in a new style and caught it up with combs.

I went down into the kitchen to see if there was anything in the refrigerator I could nibble on while I was waiting for Blake. I was starving and I wasn't used to waiting until eight o'clock to eat.

"Where are you heading to tonight?" Rose Marie asked.

"The Lobster House. Have you heard of it?"

"Of course I've heard of it, but I wager my New England clam chowder is better than theirs."

"I'm sure it is," I agreed, selecting a piece of fried chicken.

"Isn't this your weekend to go home?"

"Mrs. Beaumont said I could have it off, but I think I'll stay here instead of going home."

"Oh, I see. You don't want to let Blake out of your sight," Rose Marie observed.

"My parents may still be traveling," I answered.

"I'm glad your dad found work. Times are tough. It hurts a man's pride to be out of a job."

I went outside and waited on the steps of the veranda that ran the length of the house and dripped with hanging plants. Big urns of geraniums and trailing vinca vine flanked each side of the steps. I had pretended to be a guest at this spacious summer home so long that I almost believed I was one. I tried to imagine how it would be to grow up in a world of servants, big homes, and fast cars. Of course, the rich had their problems, too, but it would be nice not to worry about money.

Blake drove up in his car and I ran out to meet him. He gave me a disarming smile. "You look wonderful. I like the way you're wearing your hair." He had on a blue shirt, as blue as his eyes.

"How far is the Lobster House?" I asked as I slid into the seat beside him.

"About ten miles up the coast. What's wrong? Are you hungry?"

"Starved."

"Be sure and order the lobster. I don't have to tell you it's the specialty of the house," Blake said.

"Sounds good." I had never eaten lobster but I wouldn't admit it.

He held out a hand. "Come closer. I want you near to me." He had one hand on the wheel and the other covered mine. I was so conscious of the weight and warmth of his hand.

The Lobster House was built out over the water and the outside looked unpretentious. Inside, soft music, the hum of conversation, and the tinkle of glasses greeted us in an elegant setting. As we waited for the hostess, a couple at a table waved to us.

"There're Jerome and Gina," Blake said, leading me over to the table. A dark-haired boy with glasses sat with a deeply tanned girl. Her long, blond hair was almost white and she had a preppy, health-food look. I was sure she was into yoga and meditation, too.

"Jerome and Gina, I'd like you to meet Shannon. She's staying with the Beaumonts this summer," Blake said.

"I've seen you on the beach with the little boys," Gina remarked, and I felt a sense of foreboding as I sat down. Then she ignored me and turned to Blake. "What have you been doing this summer? I didn't have a chance to talk to you long at the Beaumont party. You suddenly disappeared."

"You knew my brother and I went out West on our bikes," Blake answered. "We covered nearly thirty-five hundred miles and went as far west as the Dakotas."

"Man, I would have liked to have been along!" Jerome said, "but my dad had this crazy idea I should work on the newspaper this summer."

"Don't knock it," Blake replied. "You'll probably own the newspaper someday."

"I don't want the family business. I'm interested in politics," Jerome answered. "Gina, here, is working in the art museum this summer."

"I'll be working next summer, too," Blake said. "This is my last summer for goofing off. Have you ordered yet?"

"No, we just got here."

The waiter finally came over to take our orders and we all ordered lobster. While we were waiting to be served Jerome said to me, "You know Blake and I will be rooming together at college this fall?"

"Yes. Blake told me."

"I'll try to keep an eye on him for you but he's popular with the girls. My brother gave me some great advice. He said to go to the freshman girls' dorm and tell them you're the student building inspector and warn them not to make any holes in the walls to hang their junk. Ask them for their names and telephone numbers because you will be calling back to see if they've complied with regulations. That way we can get the telephone numbers of the most interesting girls."

"If you have to do that to meet girls, I think it's sad," Gina said.

Blake smiled at me. "I don't need any girls' telephone numbers." It made me feel good to hear him say that in front of Gina and Jerome.

Gina yawned. "Don't start telling the pranks you and Blake used to play at Phillips Academy. It's very boring."

"It's *Deerfield* Academy, Gina, and we wouldn't dream of boring you," replied Blake, drily.

Our salads came, and as I ate mine I noticed that Gina seemed to be studying me. I felt uncomfortable. I wondered if I was using the right fork.

"Shannon goes to Sunderlin's," Blake said.

"Oh, really," Gina answered with a little smile.

Blake asked, "Didn't your sister go there, Gina?"

"Yes, Kelly spent two years at Sunderlin's. What year are you, Shannon?" Gina asked.

"A senior." I seemed to hear a little warning bell clanging in my head.

"How interesting," Gina continued. "Tell me, do they still sneak into the laundry room at night for beer blasts?"

"Yes." I felt like a guppy who has been tossed into a fish tank with a piranha.

"Can you still hire a cab and sneak out

after eleven P.M.?" The little smile was still there.

"Sure, no problem." My mouth felt dry.

"What dormitory will you be living in?" Gina continued.

I was trapped and my color mounted. "I . . . I'm not sure."

"That's strange. They usually notify the seniors by mail in the summer," she said.

The waiter came with our dinners and I stared at the whole lobster in front of me. I had no idea how to tackle it. It lay red and hideous on my plate as if daring me to touch it. Gina had upset me and I was so nervous my hands shook. I was sure Gina was watching me.

I couldn't hesitate any longer. I picked up my knife and fork and bore down hard on the shell. Suddenly, the lobster slipped from under my knife and went skidding across the table and onto the floor.

There was an embarrassed silence; I wished I could die right then and there. Without a word, Blake picked up the lobster with his napkin and signaled the waiter. I was so mortified I excused myself and fled to the ladies' room.

Alone, I held my hands over my flushed face. I'd made a fool of myself in front of Blake and his friends, and I was sure Blake regretted ever bringing me here. There was a touch of class to everything Blake did, and I turned out to be about as classy as a bad joke.

To my dismay, Gina had followed me into

the ladies' room. She took a comb out of her purse and began combing her long hair while watching me in the mirror. Had she said anything to Blake?

Finally, she turned and faced me. "I wonder where they will put you up at Sunderlin's this fall. The school closed two years ago."

I felt an anguished desperation. My only hope was to keep my cool and bluff my way out of this. I took my lipstick out of my purse and tried to apply it with a shaky hand. "The whole thing is a joke. I'm going to tell Blake the truth."

"About what?"

"Where I go to school."

"Why didn't you tell him in the first place? Are you ashamed? Do you have a reputation there?"

Let Gina believe that if she wanted to. "I'd rather not talk about it."

She looked interested. "Did you get kicked out?"

"I said, I'd rather not talk about it."

Gina's eyes narrowed. "Besides, you're the baby-sitter at the Beaumonts'. My mother plays golf with Janice Beaumont and she told her about the girl she had hired."

I answered with the quick tongue of a guilty conscience. "I said I'd tell Blake the truth. I didn't commit a federal offense. It's just a joke."

"I don't know what you're trying to pull, but Blake happens to be a friend of Jerome's and mine and I don't want him to be made a fool of. I hate phonies!"

"Haven't you got a sense of humor?" I retorted, still bluffing.

"It's a pretty bad joke and I don't want to be a part of it."

I almost begged her. "Go along with me, please! Just for tonight."

She looked me straight in the eye. "I don't owe you a thing. You'd better tell him soon or I will!"

There was nothing to do but follow Gina back to the table. I couldn't hide in the ladies' room all evening.

"Hey, don't look so glum, Shannon," Jerome said when we sat down at the table. "Anyone can have an accident. It's not the end of the world."

"I ordered you another lobster. It will be here shortly," Blake said. I knew I had embarrassed him.

"Please, don't wait for me," I answered. "Your food will get cold."

"We'll wait," Blake answered.

"I'm really not hungry," I insisted. "A bowl of clam chowder will be fine."

"Don't be a martyr," Jerome advised. "It's not becoming."

"Leave her alone!" Blake ordered.

"Well, we don't burn people at the stake for committing a faux pas in a restaurant," Jerome added.

"Are you afraid to tackle another lobster?" Gina asked.

"Shut up, both of you!" Blake demanded. "I'll show you how it's done, Shannon." My steaming lobster arrived and Blake showed me how to crack the shell to get at the meat. I made a halfhearted attempt to eat but there was such a lump in my throat I could hardly swallow.

Gina ignored me completely for the rest of the dinner, which didn't go unnoticed by Blake. He tried to include me in the conversation, but I was too nervous to participate. She kept referring to good times the three of them had had in the past in an effort to block me out completely.

Gina can't wait to tell Jerome about me, I thought. And, of course, Jerome will tell Blake. That's what good friends are for — to let you know when someone is making a fool of you. Unless I told Blake the truth tonight, he would find out through this unpleasant girl. It was an awful situation to be in, but it was all my own fault.

When we paid the bill Jerome said, "Do you want to follow us to Gandy's or ride in my car?"

Blake put an arm around me. "If you don't mind, I think Shannon and I would like to be alone tonight."

Jerome protested, "I thought we were going to make a night of it."

"Some other time," Blake answered.

"Come on, Jerome," Gina said. "Can't you see we aren't wanted?" She smiled her little smile. "Give my regards to the faculty at Sunderlin's. If you can locate any of them."

"What did she mean by that crack?" Blake asked as we got in the car. "Was there a mass exodus of the faculty?"

136

"I guess you could call it that." I hated myself.

He started the car and backed out of the parking lot. "I didn't like Gina's attitude. I had about all I could take of her for one night. Who does she think she is, anyway? I don't know what Jerome sees in her. She's been miserable ever since she was a kid."

I didn't answer and we drove for a way in silence. "What would you like to do tonight?" he asked. "See a show? Take in a movie?"

"It doesn't matter," I said dejectedly.

"Don't start acting weird again, Shannon. Are you still upset over the lobster?"

"Wouldn't you be?" I asked.

"Worse things can happen in a restaurant. How do you think a waitress feels when she drops food on a customer or a guy forgets his wallet?"

"That's different. I embarrassed you."

"It was no big deal. Now, let's forget it. I asked Ryan this morning if he would sail with me in the race next weekend and he agreed."

"I thought he would. He seemed pleased you asked him," I replied.

"Do you think it was tacky of me to ask him? I know how he feels about you," Blake said.

"No, I think he really wants to race."

"It's been years since we sailed together. We'll have to make some practice runs next week," Blake answered.

As we drove along the shore, I watched the lights of the boats on the water. How much longer did I have with Blake? Would Jerome tell him about me tomorrow or the next day? Even if my luck held out and he didn't hear of it from Jerome, in a little more than a week I would have to leave Piedmont Point and return home.

Blake talked about college and I knew he was looking forward to starting. The truth was that during the past week my thoughts were also turning toward going back to school. I wondered who my homeroom teacher would be and if my friends would be in my classes — would we have a good football team this year and would I be elected to the student council? The last days of August are like that — you begin thinking of your life in the fall. The rhythm of your life changes as the days slip into autumn.

Blake parked the car along a stretch of dunes and turned off the lights. The night air was cool; I shivered and held my arms.

"Are you cold, Shannon?"

"A little. It gets damp when the sun goes down."

"I'll warm you," he said, gathering me in his arms. He was at his most romantic best, and his kisses melted my resolve to reveal that I was only the Beaumonts' baby-sitter. My grandmother used to refer to silly people who lived just for today as "living in a fool's paradise," and that aptly described me. The wonder that someone like Blake could love me blanked out any good sense I might have had.

* * *

The suspense was terrible and I waited all week for Blake to confront me with my lies. But he was still his pleasant, self-confident self. The week passed all too quickly. When Ryan had time off he and Blake took the *Algonquin* out for practice runs on the bay and I sat on the beach and watched them. I began to resent the sailboat as it was consuming all Blake's attention. We played tennis a few evenings and attended a country fair, but all Blake could talk about was the race.

Jamie joined me on the beach one day and we watched the sailboat ride the waves. "Did you buy any new clothes for school, Shannon?"

"A plaid skirt and two sweaters," I answered. "Clothes are so expensive here. I'll probably wait until I get home to get what else I need."

"Prices drop dramatically after the tourists leave, even in the better boutiques, and you can get some good buys. Many of the little shops close November first for the winter season."

I ran my hands through my hair. "My hair has gotten so dry from the sun and salt water. I should have the ends trimmed, too. It's getting straggly. Do you know of a good beauty shop?"

"I'll cut your hair," she offered.

I looked doubtful.

She smiled, "Relax. I'm taking beauty culture at school. I'll just trim it a little. A blunt cut would look neater than those straggly ends and an oil treatment would put back the sheen. I give myself one every two weeks. The salt water is murder on your hair."

I'm particular about my hair and it took some urging before I agreed to let her cut it. I've lived through some bad haircuts, but Jamie promised to only take off an inch. We made plans for the next day, which was Thursday and my day off.

Jamie lived over the bakery in town with her mother, who was divorced, and her younger sister. In a corner of her crowded bedroom, which she shared with her sister, she had a floor model dryer and an array of bottles of shampoos, hair conditions, and lotions. "Are you going to take up beauty culture professionally?" I asked.

"I really don't know. Right now, I do my mother's and sister's hair and fool around with my own. I've given some of my friends body waves."

Under my critical eye she trimmed off the ends of my hair. I admitted it was an improvement. We talked while she gave me the oil treatment, and I told her about the lobster dinner and the confrontation I had had with Gina.

Jamie placed a plastic cap over my head. "Gina is a troublemaker. I don't trust her."

My voice showed my concern. "I don't understand why Jerome or Gina haven't said anything to Blake yet."

"Gina's family leaves Piedmont Point at least a week before Labor Day to get the younger children ready for school. I know because I've baby-sat for them. Maybe Gina left with her parents." She tucked a few stray strands of hair under the cap. "Jerome may wait until he and Blake are rooming together in college before he says anything."

I couldn't believe my luck was still holding out. It might get me past Labor Day.

Jamie took a broom and swept the hair clippings on the floor into a dust pan. "It's none of my business . . . but wouldn't you rather he heard it from you?"

"Of course I would . . . but the time is never right." My voice trailed away like the wisps of fog that vanish over the bay.

Jamie stopped sweeping and leaned on the broom. "Excuses, excuses! Don't you know you can't win this one, Shannon?"

I spoke sharply, "If Blake is angry that I'm the baby-sitter, then he's nothing but a snob."

She resumed her sweeping. "Are you sure you're not the snob?"

"What do you mean?"

"Isn't the glamour surrounding Blake part of his attraction — the wealthy family, the prestigious life-style?"

I was offended. "You're not being fair!"

"Suppose Ryan's and Blake's roles were reversed and it was Ryan who had all the advantages. Would that make Ryan more attractive to you?"

"I know what you must think of me, Jamie, but I love Blake. I've never felt this way about a boy before."

"Then I feel sorry for you," she answered.

CHAPTER TWELVE _____

On Friday afternoon Scott and Robbie were playing on the porch with their leap-frog game and Scott called to me, "Shannon, will you play with me? Robbie doesn't wait his turn and he hits the frogs instead of catching them with his net."

"I win!" Robbie exclaimed.

"I think he's a little young to understand the game," I said to Scott. Then I turned to Robbie. "I'll play a game with Scott and you watch."

"Scott cheat!" Robbie answered.

Scott scoffed, "He doesn't even know what cheating is!"

I played a few games with Scott. Robbie decided he was bored and went down the steps to watch the ants on the sidewalk. Suddenly, Scott exclaimed, "Here comes Blake!"

Blake came jogging along the sidewalk and took the steps two at a time. "Have you seen the evening paper?"

"No. What's happening?" Our evening paper lay neatly folded on the porch.

"The picture you entered won second prize!" He opened the paper and there was the picture of Scott and Robbie examining the sand dollar. Below the caption, "The Wonder of It All," was my name and address, followed by the boys' names and their parents' name and address.

"I don't believe it!" I cried.

Scott came to the door and shouted to his mother, "Our picture is in the newspaper! Come and see it!"

Mrs. Beaumont appeared at the door, a puzzled expression on her face, "What do you mean, Scott? Why would your picture be in the paper?"

As Blake spread the nespaper before her, I saw her color rise. She turned on me. "How dare you enter my children's picture in a newspaper contest! Don't you realize all the families here live with the fear of our children being abducted and we shun all publicity? Now you have identified our children by their picture for the whole world to view!"

I was so taken aback that I could only stammer, "I'm sorry. I would never do anything to endanger the children."

Her voice rose. "You've done nothing but cause trouble for me all summer. I'm sorry you ever came to Piedmont Point!"

Blake spoke up. "Mrs. Beaumont, Shannon meant no harm. She has watched your children all summer so you would be free to enjoy yourself. I think you have imposed on

143

Shannon and now you talk to her as if she were a criminal. This is no way to treat a guest."

"A guest!" Mrs. Beaumont sputtered. "What makes you think Shannon is our guest? We hired her as a baby-sitter!"

For one terrible moment our eyes met and I saw the hurt and disbelief in Blake's face. I turned my head away in shame. I heard him murmur an apology to Mrs. Beaumont; then he turned abruptly and went down the steps.

I wanted to throw my pride away and run after him to beg his forgiveness, but Mrs. Beaumont wasn't through with me yet. Her voice hammered at me, "To think I trusted you with my children all summer!"

"Mrs. Beaumont, I never thought the picture would win. I was just pleased Ryan Webster's teacher thought it was good enough to be entered in the contest. I understand now why you wouldn't want the picture in the paper."

"And to deceive Blake Harrison all summer into thinking you were our guest! What must his parents think of me! I'll be ashamed to face them. It's a good thing you have only three more days here or I'd tell you to pack your things!"

I said quietly, "I'll leave now if you want me to."

"Indeed not. You'll work your week out if you expect to be paid. We have a lot of packing to do for our return to Boston."

Finally she let me go. I ran up to my room and closed the door. I felt too numb to cry

144

and I paced back and forth, occasionally catching a glimpse of my drawn face, my eyes darkened with self-incrimination. My deception had ended in the worst possible way; I had hurt Blake and destroyed the love and trust he had for me. I was getting just what I deserved. But the hardest thing I had to deal with was that I had hurt Blake.

The summer had been both the happiest and the most painful of my life. Could Blake forgive me? Would he make allowance for my foolishness — or was my betrayal of his trust unforgivable? I remembered our long afternoons on the beach, the picnic on the little island, the trip to Provincetown where he'd bought me the opal pendant.

I stayed in my room and didn't go down to dinner. Around seven o'clock Rose Marie came upstairs with a tray. She had tried to make it attractive with a pretty blue cloth and a tea rose from the garden. I turned away from the food.

"I'm not hungry," I said.

She set the tray down on the desk where I sat trying to write a letter to Blake. "You'd better eat. Going on a hunger strike won't help matters."

"I'm not on a hunger strike. I couldn't eat a thing."

"I heard Mrs. Beaumont yelling at you, and she did have a point."

"You know I wouldn't do anything to hurt Robbie or Scott."

Rose Marie gave a rueful sort of smile. "Sure, I know that. I told Mrs. Beaumont to make allowance for you because you have never worked for wealthy people and you don't understand their problems. They worry about burglaries and kidnapping threats. The Beaumonts spent nearly six thousand dollars for an elaborate security system here and in their Boston home."

I didn't answer. I just wanted to be alone.

She continued, "Mrs. Beaumont was just as upset about the Harrisons. You've embarrassed her by telling Blake you were a guest here."

I put my head down on the desk. Her voice softened. "You didn't expect it to end any other way, did you, honey?"

I hadn't cried all afternoon or evening but I began to cry now, my tears making spreading blots on the blue tea cloth. I couldn't stop and Rose Marie came over and put an arm around me. "You should apologize to him, Shannon. It's the decent thing to do."

"I could never face him," I sobbed.

"Be woman enough to tell him you're sorry. The rest will be up to Blake."

Mrs. Beaumont kept me busy the next day packing the children's toys and some of their clothing. She sent me on numerous errands: to the library to return books, to the dry cleaners and the post office. I helped Rose Marie pack the china and collectibles that would be shipped back to Boston. The house would be closed the Tuesday following Labor Day.

Ryan called in the morning. "Congratulations, Shannon! Do you know, there were over two hundred entries in the contest and you copped second prize!"

"Ryan, I'd rather not talk about it. I'm in a lot of trouble with Mrs. Beaumont. She feels I endangered the security of the children when I entered the contest."

He gave a low whistle. "I never thought of that. Do you want me to have Mr. Colburn call her and explain that it was his idea?"

"No, it won't make any difference. Thanks just the same."

"I'm sorry. It was such a great picture I guess none of us realized how the Beaumonts might feel."

"I'll be leaving Labor Day and I'm sure the Beaumonts will be glad to see me go."

"You're going to watch Blake and me race tomorrow, aren't you?"

"If I can get away. What time is the race?" I asked.

"Two o'clock." He paused. "Did Blake and you have a fight? We sailed last night after supper and he never mentioned you. He seemed down."

"Maybe he had a bad day," I answered. I didn't want to tell Ryan over the phone what had happened.

It was nearly three o'clock before Mrs. Beaumont sent me to the beach with the children. She was still rigid and unforgiving and she only spoke to me when it was absolutely necessary.

I settled down on the sand with the boys, the beach ball, Poo Dog, and the pails and shovels. While the boys dug in the sand I sat hoping Blake would join me but he never showed up. In the evening I waited for him to call me but the phone didn't ring. I knew he was really hurting. It was going to be up to me to make the first move. I had never felt so lost and alone. What do you say to a boy who thinks you're special and finds out you're nothing but a phony?

It was nearly ten o'clock that evening before I summoned the courage to leave the house and walk slowly down Beach Avenue like a prisoner walking the last mile. As I neared the Harrison house I could see they were having a party. The house blazed with lights, and expensive sports cars and Cadillacs were parked in the long, curving driveway. Music drifted out into the summer night and I could hear the guests' laughter.

I stood in the shadows for a long time, trying to get myself together before going up the broad steps. Through the glass of the large bow window I could see the party inside. Was Blake in there with another girl?

At last I knocked on the door and a maid answered. "May I speak to Blake Harrison?"

"Wait here," she answered. "I'll call him." She didn't ask me to come inside.

Long minutes passed before I saw Blake coming toward me. He opened the door and stepped outside. I searched his face, hoping for a clue to tell me how he felt, but he showed no expression.

A tightness came into my throat and I stumbled over my words. "Blake, I'm sorry I lied to you. It started as a joke but it became so involved. I didn't know how to handle it."

He stood looking down at me without speaking. There was nothing to do but go on. "At first I just wanted to impress you. When I found out you cared for me" — my voice broke — "I thought it was because you believed I was a part of your world. I was afraid that if I told you the truth I would lose you."

Blake looked uncomfortable but he didn't speak. I began to cry. I felt a hand on my shoulder. "It's all right, Shannon. Please don't cry."

"I'm sorry you found out the way you did. I never meant to hurt you."

"I didn't enjoy watching Mrs. Beaumont put you down," he answered. "I think I understand why you wanted to pretend."

"That's me, the Great Pretender. Isn't that another word for liar?" I said bitterly.

"If you want to be hard on yourself." He glanced back at the party. "I have to go back in. I have friends waiting. Are you watching the race tomorrow?"

"Do you want me to?" I asked without conviction.

"Of course I do. We expect to win, you know."

I wanted so desperately to believe that my lies hadn't made any difference, that our love surmounted my mistake. Didn't everyone make mistakes? Yet I felt an uneasiness as I walked home. I almost wished Blake had shouted at me and let out his anger.

Maybe everything will be all right when Blake has more time to think it over, I thought. I had apologized, and as Rose Marie had said, the rest was up to Blake.

Jamie stopped at the house for me on Sunday afternoon, and we walked down to the docks where we could get a good view of the races. "Why are you so quiet?" Jamie asked. "Is something wrong? You look as if you've been crying."

The Visine and the cold packs on my eyes apparently hadn't helped the effects of my sleepless night, and I told her what had happened between Blake and me.

"Aren't you relieved everything is out in the open now?" Jamie asked. "How is Blake taking it?"

"It's hard to know. He just acted super cool."

Jamie sighed. "Mac would have screamed his head off if I did something like that."

"At least you would know where you stand with Mac," I answered.

"I certainly do," she laughed. "Mac's emotions are primitive."

The boats were lined up in the water and I picked out Blake's sailboat. Ryan spotted us in the crowd and waved, but if Blake knew we were there he pretended not to notice. I tried to keep track of the boat during the next two hours, but as they sailed farther away the boats looked all alike and were just white blobs on the horizon. I would have been bored if I hadn't been so worried about facing Blake again.

Later in the afternoon, when they rounded the buoys and were coming closer to shore, I sensed an excitement in the crowd. Jamie grabbed me. "Blake's in the lead! They're going to win."

"How can you tell?" I couldn't make out the figures in the lead boat.

"Here, take my binoculars," she said.

I raised the binoculars to my eyes; Ryan and Blake looked amazingly close. I wished I could reach out and touch Blake. I didn't want to give the binoculars back to Jamie. I just wanted to keep on looking at Blake because I had a strange premonition there wasn't a place for me in his life anymore.

Jamie finally took the binoculars away from me. "I want to see who's finishing second."

When Blake's boat crossed the finish line a cheer went up from the crowd. "Let's congratulate them!" Jamie said when the boys moored their boat and came ashore. I hung back but Jamie took my arm and pulled me along. I stood awkwardly at the edge of the crowd waiting for Blake to notice me, but he was laughing and talking with his friends. Jamie had run up and kissed both Ryan and Blake, and Ryan looked around for me. When he saw I was alone he came over smiling, pleased with himself, his tall frame towering above the crowd.

"Congratulations." I smiled.

"Thanks, Shannon. It was a good race and we had some stiff competition."

"I'm leaving in the morning, Ryan. I won't forget the good times we had together."

He stood looking down at me, holding his navy warm-up jacket over his shoulder. "It won't be the same with you gone."

I hated good-byes. "Thanks for everything, Ryan."

He avoided my eyes. "Well, I'd better get my things out of the boat. Good-bye, Shannon."

I watched the other boats come in, pretending interest as the names were announced over the loudspeakers, but I was so aware of Blake with his friends. Wasn't he even going to say good-bye to me?

Finally the crowd thinned, and I saw Blake coming toward me. I tried to speak lightly. "It's great to end the summer a winner."

"Thank you. I told you we would win. I couldn't have done it without Ryan."

There was an awkward pause as I tried to think of something profoundly witty to say. Then Blake said, "You're winding up your summer, too. Are you all packed?"

"Ready to go." I wasn't, really. I had been too upset to do anything.

Then Blake offered his hand. "Well, good-bye, Shannon. I'll call you sometime."

I knew he would never call. We shook hands like two business people closing a deal and when I remembered what we had meant to each other during the summer, I thought my heart would break.

Blake started to move away but I tossed my pride away and touched his arm. "Blake, would you be willing to give me another chance?"

His eyes were grave. "I don't think I could ever believe you again, Shannon." He turned and walked back to the dock.

I packed the next morning and said good-bye to Rose Marie and Scott and Robbie, who cried because I wasn't going back to Boston with them. Mr. and Mrs. Beaumont were playing golf and had left my check with Rose Marie, so I was spared the embarrassment of saying good-bye to them. Rose Marie had packed a box lunch of chicken sandwiches and chocolate brownies for me to eat on the bus.

I carried my luggage downstairs and put it on the porch. Then I went back upstairs for the bags and boxes that contained the things I had accumulated during the summer — extra clothes, souvenirs, junk. I wondered how I would get it all on the bus.

I couldn't wait to leave. Everywhere I looked reminded me of Blake, especially the beach where we had spent so many hours. My messed-up summer. The summer I hadn't done anything right. I had met a wonderful boy and lost him through my own foolishness.

I carried the last of my stuff downstairs

when I heard a car pull up. It was Ryan. "My dad said I could use the car. I'm going to drive you home."

"Ryan, you don't have to. It's ninety miles. Don't you have to work?"

"It's all taken care of. Did you really think you could get all this stuff in the bus?" he asked.

I wondered if he knew about Blake and me and I had the feeling he did. I hadn't sworn Jamie to secrecy. "I wonder why you bother with me after all the trouble I got into this summer."

"Remember you told me a friend is a person who knows all about you and still likes you? Well, that's the way it is with me. Now, let's get this baggage in the car."

We packed my things in the trunk and I turned and waved to Rose Marie, Scott, and Robbie, who were standing on the porch. I was going to miss them. Then I got into the car and we started down the road.

Out of my messed-up summer one thing remained constant — Ryan's friendship. I realized how lucky I was to have a friend like him. I stared straight ahead, without glancing at the sun-drenched beach. It was too painful to even think about it.

I was through pretending. From now on, people would have to take me as I am. I would be my own person.

As if Ryan knew what I was thinking, he turned to me and smiled. I took his hand and we drove away from Piedmont Point, back home to where I could be myself.

SUNFIRE®

Read all about the fascinating young women who lived and loved during America's most turbulent times!

☐ 32774-7		**AMANDA** Candice F. Ransom		$2.95
☐ 33064-0		**SUSANNAH** Candice F. Ransom		$2.95
☐ 33156-6		**DANIELLE** Vivian Schurfranz		$2.95
☐ 33241-4	#5	**JOANNA** Jane Claypool Miner		$2.95
☐ 33242-2	#6	**JESSICA** Mary Francis Shura		$2.95
☐ 33239-2	#7	**CAROLINE** Willo Davis Roberts		$2.95
☐ 33688-6	#14	**CASSIE** Vivian Schurfranz		$2.95
☐ 33686-X	#15	**ROXANNE** Jane Claypool Miner		$2.95
☐ 41468-2	#16	**MEGAN** Vivian Schurfranz		$2.75
☐ 41438-0	#17	**SABRINA** Candice F. Ransom		$2.75
☐ 42134-4	#18	**VERONICA** Jane Claypool Miner		$2.75
☐ 40049-5	#19	**NICOLE** Candice F. Ransom		$2.25
☐ 42228-6	#20	**JULIE** Vivian Schurfranz		$2.75
☐ 40394-X	#21	**RACHEL** Vivian Schurfranz		$2.50
☐ 40395-8	#22	**COREY** Jane Claypool Miner		$2.50
☐ 40717-1	#23	**HEATHER** Vivian Schurfranz		$2.50
☐ 40716-3	#24	**GABRIELLE** Mary Francis Shura		$2.50
☐ 41000-8	#25	**MERRIE** Vivian Schurfranz		$2.75
☐ 41012-1	#26	**NORA** Jeffie Ross Gordon		$2.75
☐ 41191-8	#27	**MARGARET** Jane Claypool Miner		$2.75
☐ 41207-8	#28	**JOSIE** Vivian Schurfranz		$2.75
☐ 41416-X	#29	**DIANA** Mary Francis Shura		$2.75
☐ 42043-7	#30	**RENEE** Vivian Schurfranz (February '89)		$2.75

Scholastic Inc., P.O. Box 7502, 2932 East McCarty Street, Jefferson City, MO 65102

Please send me the books I have checked above. I am enclosing $ _____
(please add $1.00 to cover shipping and handling). Send check or money-order—no cash or C.O.D.'s please.

Name _____

Address _____

City _____ State/Zip _____

Please allow four to six weeks for delivery. Offer good in U.S.A. only. Sorry, mail order not available to residents of Canada. Prices subject to change.   **SUN 888**